The door opened and she found herself holding her breath all over again.

Paul Reyes stood in the open doorway. Cool linen slacks and pure white shirt contrasted sharply with his smooth, dark skin. "Do you care to amend your reason for showing up at my door?"

Renee was made. Might as well give it her best effort. She thrust out her hand. "It's a pleasure to meet you, Mr. Reyes."

He looked at her hand, then her. Fortunately, propriety appeared to prevent him from ignoring her gesture. His handshake was soft but firm. Dark brown eyes assessed her closely, the slightest hint of suspicion lingering there.

"What is it you desire of me?" he asked as he released her hand. "Your bold determination has intrigued me."

He was intrigued. But enough to know that he was already marked for death?

DEBRA WEBB

HOSTAGE SITUATION

HARLEQUIN®

TORONTO • NEW YORK • LONDON
AMSTERDAM • PARIS • SYDNEY • HAMBURG
STOCKHOLM • ATHENS • TOKYO • MILAN • MADRID
PRAGUE • WARSAW • BUDAPEST • AUCKLAND

This book is dedicated to Sean Mackiewicz.
Thank you for all you do.

ISBN-13: 978-0-373-69256-9
ISBN-10:   0-373-69256-0

HOSTAGE SITUATION

www.eHarlequin.com

Printed in U.S.A.

ABOUT THE AUTHOR

Debra Webb was born in Scottsboro, Alabama, to parents who taught her that anything is possible if you want it bad enough. She began writing at age nine. Eventually, she met and married the man of her dreams, and tried various occupations, including selling vacuum cleaners, and working in a factory, a daycare center, a hospital and a department store. When her husband joined the military, they moved to Berlin, Germany, and Debra became a secretary in the commanding general's office. By 1985 they were back in the States, and finally moved to a small town in Tennessee, where everyone knows everyone else. With the support of her husband and two beautiful daughters, Debra took up writing again, looking to mystery and movies for inspiration. In 1998, her dream of writing for Harlequin Books came true. You can write to Debra with your comments at P.O. Box 64, Huntland, Tennessee 37345 or visit her Web site at www.debrawebb.com to find out exciting news about her next book.

Books by Debra Webb

HARLEQUIN INTRIGUE

CAST OF CHARACTERS

Jim Colby—The head of the Equalizers and the son of Victoria Colby-Camp. Jim needs a fresh start.

Victoria Colby-Camp—The head of the Colby Agency. Victoria wants the best for her son even if it means he doesn't come to work for her.

Tasha Colby—Jim's wife and the mother of their daughter Jamie.

Renee Vaughn—A former prosecutor. She is ready to stop playing it so straight and safe and start infusing some danger into her life. She just didn't expect it to come with attachments.

Paul Reyes—His work is his life. He wants nothing to do with the evil monster his brother has become. If he is to survive, he will need help. He did not anticipate that help from a beautiful woman.

Victor Reyes—He wants his brother's life in order to save his own. The only variable is how many people he will have to kill to suceed.

Joseph Gates—DEA Agent Gates has a personal stake in stopping Victor Reyes.

Sam Johnson—The grittiest new associate at the Equalizers. Don't mess with Sam—or you might find yourself dead.

Chapter One

"Stop the car!"

Renee Vaughn shoved a fistful of cash at the taxi driver and scrambled out of the car. She sucked in deep, ragged gulps of air…still unable to get enough oxygen into her lungs. Her body shook with the news that had chilled her to the bone.

It's not right.

The judicial system had failed.

She had failed.

The execution would not be stayed.

At midnight, an innocent man would die, and there was nothing she could do to help him.

Nausea roiled in her stomach. She took the few steps across the sidewalk to brace herself against the nearest building. She closed her eyes and tried to block the painful memories churning in her head.

She was a murderer.

The sounds of evening's rush-hour traffic filtered through the haze of emotions, ushering back time and place. Renee forced her eyes open and blinked to focus.

She'd been down this road already. This wasn't her problem any more. She should go home, put it out of her mind. She'd been taken off the case two years ago. Her former client's new attorney had taken out a restraining order to ensure she kept her distance.

There was every reason for her to forget…to put the whole damned mess behind her.

But she couldn't. The man sitting on death row awaiting execution was her brother. She knew the truth, or at least part of it, and he would not allow her to stop this. No one would listen to her.

The wind whipped around her, urging her to move…to pull herself together. She glanced around to get her bearings. Madison Street. She could walk home from here. Her place wasn't more than ten blocks away. Her legs still felt a little unsteady, but she'd be okay just as soon as the initial shock wore off.

Her gaze landed on St. Peter's. Of all places for her to decide she needed out of the confines of the taxi. Before the thought could completely evolve in her brain, she was walking through the door. She couldn't remember the last time she'd been in church. Or the last time she'd prayed, for that matter.

Her mind in a chaotic battle of emotion against reason, she moved up the aisle between the rows of pews, her movements on autopilot. She approached the chapel at the back of the church and knelt in front of the icon. She lit a single candle, offered a silent prayer for the innocent man who would die a few hours from now. It would take a miracle to save her brother now and, as an attorney and former prosecutor, she knew better than to believe in miracles. Her chest constricted and a flood of tears pressed against the backs of her eyes.

Her mistake. No matter what anyone said, she knew where the fault lay.

She didn't have to be present in Huntsville, Texas, to imagine the scene. A crowd would be gathered already. Newspaper and television journalists from across the state. Protesters, those for and against the death penalty, with their signs and chants. The family members of victims, anticipating the moment when a convicted killer would finally pay the price for his crimes.

Renee rose from the kneeler and slumped onto the front pew and sat there for a while, thankful for the anonymity and silence in the empty church. She should go home. In another hour, the church would be filled with parishioners attending Mass. But somehow she couldn't find the strength to haul herself up and walk out the door. Instead, she sat there and stared at the flame. Reaching up with a shaky hand, she ruthlessly brushed back the lone tear that managed to escape her stronghold.

"Damn it," she muttered, then immediately railed at herself for the slip.

Why should she punish herself for the actions of others? Her brother had caused this. She had tried to stop it once she knew the truth, but he had not allowed her to do the right thing. That was masochistic. She had promised herself that with this new move, she would not permit the past to take over her life again. If only someone would tell that to her foolish emotions.

A hand settled on her shoulder. Startled, she glanced up to find Jim Colby standing in the aisle. "You trying to beat the rush?" he asked.

She straightened, cleared her throat. Having him appear here was about as unexpected as finding herself at this church. He moved around her and lowered himself onto the pew scarcely an arm's length away. How could he sneak up on her so effortlessly? When had she so completely lost her edge? She blinked back the new burning tears. She would not let him see this kind of fragility. This display of weakness was not who she was. She had to get back on track.

"Ensures the best seat in the house," she said, playing along and forcing a tight smile. Don't think about it anymore. There is nothing you can do. Focus on now. What was Jim doing here? She wouldn't have taken him for a guy who bothered with Mass. Even so, that wouldn't be his reason for showing up like this. Her new boss was not a happenstance kind of guy. He was focused, intense, deliberate.

Jim smiled that slow, half tilt that she'd come to associate with him. She got the distinct impression that smiling was not typical of him, though he seemed to like to do it more and more as time went by. She'd been working for Jim Colby for a couple of months now. He was different—edgy, almost dangerous. Case in point: those penetrating blue eyes. Eyes that kept folks on their toes in his presence. Not that she was intimidated by her boss, but on some instinctive level she understood that he was not a man to be taken lightly.

"How'd you know I was here?" The idea that he would have followed her from the office didn't seem plausible.

"The mechanic dropped off your car."

Her car? She deflated a little more. How could she have forgotten about that? "Oh…I—" She gave her head a shake. "I was supposed to call to see if it would be ready." The mechanic had picked up her car at the office that morning with a simple instruction: call before leaving for the day to see if it's ready. But then, that had been before she'd got the news that the stay of execution had been denied.

Don't think about it.

"Since you hadn't made it home and weren't answering your cell, I called the cab company. Dispatcher said the driver dropped you off here. I thought I'd come give you a ride back to the office to pick up your car."

Her cell…it was on Silent. She nodded her understanding, still a little rattled. "I appreciate that." She had a feeling there was more to this than just letting her know her car was ready.

As if she'd voiced the thought aloud, his gaze locked with hers. "We have a new client. The job's going to require a somewhat dicey field assignment. At least a few days on location." He studied her for a moment, then added, "I was thinking you might be right for this one, if you feel you're ready."

Renee sat up straighter. She'd been waiting for this opportunity. She moistened her lips, swallowed at the emotion still hovering in the back of her throat. "I'm ready." No way was she going to let the past mess this up. The call she'd received less than one hour ago echoed unnervingly, but she pushed it away. Her brother's mistakes and decisions weren't her problem anymore...hadn't been in two years. She couldn't change what was going to happen...no matter how wrong. *He* had seen to that.

"I know you've been anticipating your first field assignment," Colby said.

Admittedly, running background checks and following up on cheating spouses was not how she'd seen things going at her new job. Still, paying one's dues was not a new concept to her. "I'm confident the past couple of months aren't an accurate measure of what's to come." Despite having changed jobs twice in the past two years, even she had her limits on how low she would take her career expectations.

"This one may be a little tricky."

Their gazes met. Anticipation hummed inside her.

"Tricky?" She tried to glean something from his expression, but it was impossible. Jim Colby was far too good at camouflaging whatever was on his mind.

"There could be complicating factors."

Complicating factors? She didn't have a problem with complications. In fact, she had more of a problem with a lack of them; it gave her too much free time to allow the past to invade her present. She tamped down the ache that instantly attempted to intrude. If Jim was worried about her ability to defend herself, he shouldn't be. She'd faced physical threat in the past and she'd learned from it. A comprehensive self-defense class should be mandatory for all attorneys and prosecutors.

"What kind of complicating factors?" she ventured.

"This one means you'd have to take on a whole new identity and deliberately mislead a man in order to lure his only brother into a trap."

Her curiosity spiked, sending a surge of adrenaline roaring through her veins. She'd been looking for just this sort of case. Something out of the ordinary. Something exciting...dangerous. The last startled her just a little. Would living on the edge help her put the past more firmly behind her? Make her trust herself again?

Only one way to find out.

"When do I start?"

He studied her, his eyes searching hers for some glimpse of uncertainty or maybe hesitation. She allowed none. She knew betrayal and deceit intimately. Using that painfully gained knowledge to get the job done wouldn't be a problem. If someone innocent got hurt…who cared, right? As long as the job got done and the case got closed…the end justified the means.

"It may be necessary for you to, let's just say, get very close to the target," he countered. "Are you sure you can do that, Vaughn? I'm certain that kind of deception wasn't one of your electives at that fancy law school you attended."

She did the smiling this time. "You're right. It wasn't. I had to learn that part the hard way. Now, when do I start?"

"Now."

Perfect.

He went on, "You can look over the file tonight and we'll get started on your cover profile first thing in the morning." He pushed to his feet. "That way you can catch an afternoon flight and jump right in."

"Do we have photos? Background histories?" Renee stood, genuflected and fell into step next to him as he moved down the long center aisle.

"Photos, histories. We have it all. Our client came prepared."

"Excellent." That would speed up the process. If he wanted her on a plane in less than twenty-four hours, getting up to speed ASAP would be essential.

As Renee climbed into Jim's car, she checked her

cell phone. Two missed calls and one voice mail. One of the calls was from Jim. The second had her heart thumping as she listened to the accompanying voice mail. The first three words of the message had her sagging against the seat with relief in spite of her determination not to care.

The governor called.

The stay of execution had been granted.

Renee stared out at the busy street surrounded by the eclectic architecture that set the city of Chicago apart from any other on the globe.

This was good news.

And just like that, the past nudged its way back into her life, starting the cycle of obsession and denial all over again.

Key Largo
Wednesday, May 2, 2:00 p.m.

"IT'S A FORTRESS."

A fortress. Yes. Renee studied the three-story home through binoculars from her position aboard the *Salty Dog*, a for-hire touring vessel. The two-acre estate of which her guide spoke was located on a desirable shore with not one, but two magnificent vessels—a speed boat and an enviable-sized yacht—moored at the private dock. The residence reminded her more of a compound than a home. Not exactly the sort of place one expected to find a self-professed starving artist. Though his work was well known in the southeastern region, he was no Picasso.

"Concrete walls. High-tech security system." Her guide pushed up his Miami Dolphins cap and scratched his head. "A nightmare, logistically speaking, if you're planning an unexpected *visit*."

Renee lowered the binoculars and slid her sunglasses back into place. She'd spun quite a tale to explain her need to do this type of surveillance. Thankfully, her guide had accepted her bitter story of betrayal and hadn't asked any more questions. At least her past experience had allowed her to sound genuine. "I don't see any security personnel." It was possible a bodyguard or guards were inside, but one would think guards would do routine rounds of the property. Maybe the security system was so state-of-the-art that walk-arounds weren't necessary.

"He doesn't have any bodyguards. At least not that anyone has ever spotted." Henry Napier shot her a look that suggested he was as befuddled by the idea as she. "No one can figure out that part. He drives a Maserati GranSport that cost six figures. That's new, by the way. So's the yacht." He gestured to the property that could easily be showcased in the glitziest of lifestyle magazines. "With all that you'd think he would be afraid to go to sleep at night without at least one bodyguard, but, apparently, he isn't."

Typically a man of such means would have personal security. But the man who lived in that house was no typical homeowner. She turned her attention back to the estate worth at least five million. Paul Reyes was the younger brother of Victor Reyes, a drug lord whose own compound was so carefully protected that only his closest confidants knew its location somewhere in Mexico. The concept that Paul lived so openly and clearly unprotected just didn't fit with the facts known about his older brother.

"This is as close as I can take you," Napier said. "City regulations. The rich folks don't like us getting too close. You still have another hour left on your tour. You want to just sit here?"

Renee didn't answer right away. She was too focused on the idea of the man beyond those well-fortified walls. Her target, Paul Reyes. Quiet, withdrawn, a mystery. That was pretty much all anyone knew about him, other than the artwork he sold through a local gallery. She'd stopped this morning at the gallery and looked at his work up close and in person. He was good, no question.

What made this man the polar opposite of his older brother? By all reports, Victor was cruel and vengeful. He had achieved his fame and fortune by taking advantage of the weaknesses of others. He didn't care who was hurt or what damage he caused to society as a whole. He cared only for himself. No one—not a single law enforcement agency—had ever come close to taking him down.

The client, Darla Stewart, who had hired the Equalizers, was the sister of a murdered New Orleans narcotics detective. Victor Reyes was responsible for her brother's death. The police and even the DEA had failed to get this guy for using New Orleans, among other seaside cities, as ports of entry for the evil he spread. When Stewart's brother, Detective Chris Nelson, had made stopping Reyes his personal quest, he'd been squashed and pushed aside like a pesky fly.

Desperate to bring her brother's killer to justice, Stewart had sought out the one man her brother had insisted he trusted in all this, DEA Agent Joseph Gates. According to Gates, he had a solid case built against Reyes for his drug crimes, but Mexico refused to acknowledge his existence, which rendered the extradition request invalid. According to the Mexican authorities, they didn't even know Victor Reyes, much less where he lived. That was possible, but it was far more probable that law enforcement south of the border had been paid off. Money could buy most anything, especially in a country such as Mexico, where poverty prevailed among the masses.

For Renee, the assignment was simple. She would use Paul Reyes as bait for luring his older brother onto American soil. Agent Gates and the DEA would take things from there. Until then, the agent's hands were tied. The DEA had spent endless resources monitoring the movements of Victor's brother here in Florida, his single connection to the U.S., with absolutely no results. With numerous other cases popping up every day, resources were already too thin. Reyes, until he appeared on American soil or the Mexican government changed its mind about extradition, was no longer a priority. Darla Stewart had been devastated when the Reyes case was put on a back burner by the DEA. With no other options, she had gone to the Equalizers for help. Agent Gates had promised to help in spite of his orders to refocus his energy, but ultimately there was nothing he could do until Victor Reyes entered his jurisdiction. All Renee had to do was make that happen.

Sounded like a piece of cake. But there was a hitch. The setup had to be legit as much as possible. Since Paul Reyes surely wouldn't be game for co-operating, then the trickery used to gain his unwitting assistance had to be on the up-and-up. Gates didn't want any snares to serve as reason to have his case torn apart by a team of legal eagles. Renee understood exactly how the legal system worked and how it could be twisted to serve an incomprehensible purpose. She had always won her cases. Even when she should have lost. She'd been set up by someone she trusted. That wouldn't happen again in this lifetime.

Though she had an understanding of sorts with Jim Colby, and she respected him, she would never totally let down her guard to him or anyone else. Complete trust was out of the question. She wouldn't be going there again. Hell, she didn't even trust herself beyond a certain degree, so how could she possibly trust anyone else? She'd trusted her former boss and mentor and he'd let her down.

She pushed the troubling thoughts away. No rehashing the bitter lessons of the past.

"Thanks, Mr. Napier. We can go back now. I've seen enough."

The old man nodded as he prepared to turn the vessel about. After her arrival late yesterday, she'd been told that Napier was the man to go to for the lowdown on island residents. Napier was a Key Largo native. He loved retelling island lore and made it his mission to keep up on the most famous and/or infamous residents. Judging by his weathered skin, the man had spent most of his life floating about these waters spying on those who made the exotic locale home. She had not been in the least disappointed by her guide.

The sun and wind and water made her feel more alive than she had in a very long while, she realized as they journeyed back to the dock lined with touring vessels. Or maybe it was the case. Working undercover like this was a first for her. Most of her time in her former career had been spent in an office or library doing research and prep work with witnesses, or in the courtroom arguing her case. This was definitely a change for the better. It felt far more purposeful.

It gave her the opportunity to be someone else.

She'd left her uptight—as her Equalizers colleague Sam Johnson called them—business suits in

Chicago. For this assignment, her first actual field-work, she'd chosen to dress as the natives did. Casual and sexy. She had the figure for it; she'd simply never had the desire. A conservative mentality had gone along with her previous career, at least on a personal level. She'd been anything but reserved in the courtroom.

She'd been good, damn it. She just hadn't been smart enough to see what was coming that one time.

Again, she ordered the memories away.

Back on shore, she generously compensated her guide and climbed into her rental car. She drove directly to her hotel. The cool air inside her room was a much-appreciated respite from the Florida heat. She turned on a light and retrieved her file from its hiding place inside the ventilation return in her room.

She considered the picture of the Reyes brothers. Victor was thirty-eight, with dark hair and eyes. If she were casting a thriller with a drug lord as the villain, he would definitely fit the bill. As handsome as he was, there was an air of menace about him. Partly posture, but mainly the way he looked directly into the camera seemingly daring anyone to cross him. She'd seen his kind before, usually stationed at the defendant's bench.

Paul, on the other hand, appeared quiet and utterly calm, harmless. Though he had been blessed with those same dark good looks, there was a serenity about him that spoke of intelligence and patience. Just two years younger than his brother, the two were, according to the reports she'd read, vastly different. Victor lived by the old rules, where women were nothing more than chattels and anything less than absolute loyalty from his followers was punishable by death. Conversely, Paul lived a quiet, reclusive life with hardly any contact with others.

The brothers had parted ways nearly a decade ago when Paul reportedly got fed up with his brother's evil deeds and came to live full-time in the United States. Be that as it may, the family blood money, in Renee's opinion, had to have purchased the lavish estate where he lived. As good as his artwork was, Paul hadn't made the leap into mainstream popularity yet.

Renee put the file away and dressed for the next step in her plan. Cream-colored slacks, a matching silk blouse and strappy but practical sandals. In her purse, she had the owner's card from the gallery she'd visited that morning. As far as she could tell, Paul rarely ventured from his estate for anything other than, in very rare instances, a gallery opening or a showing of his work. Even a large showing was no guarantee the artist would be in attendance.

That left her only one option—go to him.

She took the .22 from the box of long-stemmed roses that had been delivered by Jim Colby's contact here in Key Largo. After strapping on the ankle holster, she snugged the weapon into position. If she was lucky, she wouldn't have to use it; but if the past was any indication, luck wouldn't be anywhere around when she needed it most.

6:00 p.m.

OCEAN BOULEVARD was, as the name suggested, flanked by gorgeous sapphire water and dotted by enormous mansions. Near the end of the boulevard, where the most magnificent of the homes reigned over much larger portions of land, Renee pulled up in front of the massive iron gates of the residence belonging to Paul Reyes. She inhaled a deep, fortifying breath. Time to do this for real. She powered her window down, pressed the call button on the speaker box and then waited. Even her heart seemed to stand still as the seconds ticked by in silence.

"Yes?"

Paul Reyes. Although she had never heard his voice, the single word convinced her that it was him. The deep, velvety richness of the timbre matched the dark eyes and the quiet intensity of his face. Or maybe she just wanted it to be him, since she found the vaguely accented sound quite pleasing.

"Mr. Reyes?" She had to be sure. Her anticipation of plunging into her first case might very well be playing havoc with her reason.

"Please state your name and business."

She looked toward the camera positioned on the wall next to the gate before saying, "My name is

Renee Parsons. Mallory Rogers from the Rogers-Hall Gallery suggested I come to you in person with my intriguing proposal." Then she smiled, the most seductive one in her limited repertoire. Looking stern and purposeful was her most frequently utilized expression.

Renee held her breath now and hoped like hell her plan would work. If he called Mallory Rogers before he allowed Renee inside, she would be in trouble.

The grind of metal jolting into movement hauled her attention to the gates. Her heart jerked back into a frantic pace on the heels of an adrenaline dump. He was going to allow her in.

Anticipation roaring through her like a freight train, she took her foot off the brake pedal, and the vehicle rolled through the entrance which now yawned open. The driveway cut through a lush lawn and ended in a circular parking patio embellished by a massive center fountain.

With the vehicle in Park, she cut the engine and emerged. The air was thick and the heat hadn't subsided with the sun's descent. Before closing the door, she reached back inside and grabbed her purse and draped it over her shoulder. Inside her bag she carried a tiny listening device. Barely the size of a quarter, all she had to do was leave it in a strategic spot and she would be able to monitor his conversations in that room. Highly illegal, but a part of the way things were done in her new career.

Knowledge was power and since information on this man and his brother was seriously limited, getting what she needed this way was crucial. She had to learn all she could and burrow in as deeply as possible. Taking any and all appropriate steps to speed up the process, without being too hasty, was absolutely essential to the proper outcome.

She strolled across the lovely flagstone parking patio and up the steps that led to the front entrance. She took her time, made each step as sensual as possible as she surveyed the gorgeous property. He would be watching, and he needed to believe that she deeply appreciated beauty. Staying in character was another key element.

A wide covered portico ran the length of the house in front. She hadn't been able to see this side of the grand mansion from the water, but it definitely lived up to her expectations. She pressed the doorbell and settled her attention on the lush potted plants on either side of the towering double doors. Not a single detail had been overlooked when planning this Mediterranean-style property. All had been designed to be pleasing to the eye and equally welcoming to all the other senses.

The door opened and she found herself holding her breath all over again.

Paul Reyes stood in the open doorway. Cool linen slacks and shirt designed in pure white contrasted sharply with his smooth, dark skin. "Ms.

Rogers has no recall of recommending that anyone pay me an unannounced visit. Do you care to amend your reason for showing up at my door, Ms. Parsons?"

Oh, hell, she was made. But she was here. Might as well give it her best effort. She thrust out her hand. "It's a pleasure to meet you, Mr. Reyes."

He looked at her hand, then her. Fortunately, propriety appeared to prevent him from ignoring her gesture. He closed his hand around hers and gave it a shake. His was soft but firm. Dark brown eyes assessed her closely, the slightest hint of suspicion lingering there.

"What is it you desire of me, Ms. Parsons?" he asked as he released her hand. "Your bold determination has intrigued me."

He was intrigued. That was a start. "I'm from L.A., Mr. Reyes, and my gallery would really love to show your work. From what I've learned so far, you don't show outside Key Largo, though your work sells in several neighboring states. That's such a terrible waste of your potential. I felt the need for a face-to-face meeting any way I could get it in order to plead my case. We want Paul Reyes to become a household name on the West Coast. We can make that happen."

Jim Colby had provided a cover for her with a gallery owner friend in the Los Angeles area. That cover profile was her one ace in the hole. If it didn't work, she was on her own.

For several seconds, Paul Reyes appeared to consider her explanation carefully. There was no way to read what he was thinking, but at least he hadn't closed the door in her face.

"Do you have any credentials to prove you are who you say you are?"

Relief almost made her smile. "Certainly." She withdrew her fake California driver's license and a business card from the gallery on Melrose, each sporting the name Renee Parsons. She passed both to him for his scrutiny. She doubted anyone outside a trained professional would recognize the license was a fake, and the card was real. The owner in L.A. had overnighted a number of things to the hotel in Key Largo to help with Renee's cover.

"I have a contract proposal if you have the time to review our plan for your incredible work." The proposal, also provided by the L.A. gallery owner, she carried on a BlackBerry in her bag. "We're willing to work with you in whatever capacity you feel comfortable. We're impressed, Mr. Reyes. We want you." This part was true. Once Jim had shown the gallery in L.A. some digital images of Paul's work, they had shown interest.

"All right, Ms. Parsons." He handed her license and card back to her. "Since you've come all this way, you have half an hour. Convince me that I should consider your gallery's offer more seriously and we might be able to do business."

Half an hour. It was more than she'd hoped for.
He opened the door wider in invitation.
She was in.

Chapter Two

If Renee had thought the exterior of the house was well appointed, the interior was nothing short of lavish. Cool, sleek marble and cypress floors and soaring ceilings. From where she stood in the entry hall, she could see straight through to the endless blue of the ocean beyond a wall of towering French doors.

The floating staircase in the entry hall was at once grand and utterly modern. Somewhere inside the house the windows stood open, filling the air with the ocean's lightly salted breeze. It seemed strange to her that he would allow open windows, much less the unobstructed view from the rear of his house. Then she remembered that she hadn't been able to see in from the outside. Obviously the windows were equipped with a special tint or screening. And if the security system was half as state-of-the-art as she suspected, he likely wasn't worried about an unexpected intrusion, either.

After all, this was Paul. His brother Victor was the one who had to watch his back so closely.

"This way," he said, drawing her attention back to him. Their gazes met briefly before he turned to lead her deeper into the luxurious home.

Renee reminded herself to keep an eye on the man when her attention wanted to revel in the exquisite details around her. Evidently his artistic talent extended to his taste in design. Either that, or he'd hired himself one hell of a great interior designer.

They took a right at the grand entrance to the great room with its compelling ocean view. This side corridor provided access to several doors; he chose the second on the right—a library. The room was far too richly adorned to be called a home office. The wall of book-filled shelves lent credence to the idea of a library.

He paused in the middle of the room, looked at her and then at the purse she carried. "You mentioned a proposal," he reminded, his tone openly dubious.

"Oh, yes." She fished the BlackBerry from her purse. "It's quite an extensive proposal." She glanced around the room, her gaze landing on the computer on his desk. "I can download it if that would be more convenient." She held her breath, hoped he would go for her suggestion.

The three-second pause that followed had her heart missing a beat.

At last he swept a hand in the direction of the desk. "Be my guest."

Able to breathe again, she moved across the room to his sleek desk. She sat down, retrieved the portable cable from her purse and used it to connect her BlackBerry to his hard drive. A minute later, she had downloaded the proposal. The proposal was legitimate, but imbedded within its program was an interface that would allow her to remotely access his computer from her BlackBerry. Any files stored there might provide valuable information on his brother Victor; then again, they could very well offer nothing at all. She hoped like hell his security software wouldn't recognize the bug and work to disable it before she could accomplish her mission.

Sam Johnson, the newest associate at the Equalizers, had brought the software with him from L.A. One of the scientists he'd worked with had been a computer buff and had designed the basically invisible intruding interface to check up on what his girlfriend was doing on the Net while he worked the nightshift at the state forensics lab. He had suspected an online romance. He'd found out far more than he'd wanted to know.

"Here we go." She pushed out of his chair and gestured to the screen where the proposal portion of the program had opened to reveal the first eye-catching page. She needed him impressed.

He searched her face long enough to make her

nervous. Surely he couldn't know already that she was there under false pretenses. She hadn't made any mistakes. As nervous as she felt, on the outside she appeared calm. She wore what she considered her courtroom face.

"You must forgive my manners," he said suddenly as if he'd been lost in thought for a moment. "I so rarely have guests that I sometimes forget what is expected. Would you care for refreshments, Ms. Parsons?"

Relief rushed along her limbs. "Call me Renee," she urged before manufacturing a friendly smile. "A drink would be great." This was a move in the right direction. She needed him to feel comfortable in her presence. If only she could manage the same. The tension had ebbed a fraction, but it still had her on edge. Maybe that went with the territory.

"Why don't we attend to our thirst before we review your proposal?"

The idea that putting the proposal on his computer might have made him somewhat suspicious crossed her mind but she'd just have to play this out and see what happened. That her fingers had gone ice cold was not good. In the courtroom, she had gone in with guns blazing and had never once let the competition see her sweat. To a great extent, she was out of her element here. Her reactions weren't going to be her usual controlled responses. That was to be expected, she reminded herself. As long as she didn't let him see her fear, there was no need to stress.

Paul Reyes led the way down the corridor, beyond the entry hall to the sprawling kitchen that claimed a sizeable chunk of the downstairs floor space on the front side of the house. Gleaming stainless steel appliances maintained the modern edge, but lots of granite and tumbled marble infused an organic element. The limestone floor and wall-to-wall windows, along with the simple furnishings, ensured a casual elegance. With a deftness born of repetition, her host prepared a blend of fresh juices and garnished the concoction with sprigs of mint.

He offered a stemmed glass to her. "Far more healthy than wine."

"Thank you." She accepted the glass and sipped the blend, careful not to show her surprise at his non-alcoholic choice. "I suppose you work out, as well." He certainly looked fit. She told herself she hadn't really noticed, that making the comment was about laying the groundwork for a common physical connection, but that was only part truth. Paul Reyes was a handsome man with a deep, silky voice and just enough of an accent to make him inordinately sexy. And the body—well, there was one for the covers of the hottest magazines. She imagined that the man would look damn good in most anything or nothing at all. Getting close to him wouldn't be a chore.

"Staying fit is imperative to my image," he insisted with a blatant survey of her, from her pink toenails to her unrestrained hair. "The mind and body must be in agreement. Don't you agree?"

The way he looked at her set her further on edge. It shouldn't have. She needed him to be attracted to her. That was the point of the scoop-necked blouse and the form-fitting, low-slung slacks. But that predatory gleam in his eyes was more than she'd bargained for this early in the game. Or maybe she just hadn't expected that kind of overt reaction from a man so withdrawn in almost every other respect.

"Oh yes," she stammered. "I heartily agree."

He smiled, obviously enjoying her discomfort. "Are you one of the Los Angeles gallery's regular buyers?" he inquired. "This is what you do?"

"Actually," she heaved a beleaguered sigh and launched her well-planned story, "no. I was asked to approach you personally because I'm such a huge fan of your work. The owner is hoping my passion will prove persuasive enough to close the deal. I hate to come off as a starstruck fan, but that's exactly what I am."

If her answer moved him in any way, he kept it hidden well. Those dark eyes remained steady on her until the need to shift with uneasiness was nearly overwhelming. She held her ground, refused to allow him to see that he made her far too nervous. This was her new career. She refused to fail.

"Passion is a very powerful tool, *Renee*. In my line

of work, it is critical to all involved. One should never be ashamed of passion."

Beyond the idea of how much she liked the way he said her name, his answer brushed her senses the wrong way. Gave her pause.

My line of work.

Perhaps it was simply a matter of communication differences. After all, English was not his first language. Semantics, she argued. No need to send her suspicion radar to the next level over the way he used a couple of words. She was overanalyzing. Being nervous made her do that. Once she relaxed more fully into her role, she would be fine.

"Shall we get back to the proposal?" she prompted, needing her strict agenda to get her back on track. Her success in the courtroom was rooted, first and foremost, on extensive preparation. She needed to treat this assignment along those same lines until she hit her stride with the whole "getting comfortable" part.

He placed his half-empty glass on the island's sleek granite counter. She did the same. This time they walked side by side as they retraced the route to his library. The sun had sunk deep on the horizon, melting into a golden blanket over the vast blue ocean and offering a spectacular panorama.

The idea that drug money may have contributed to this magnificent residence caused the muscles in her jaw to tighten. But this man was not a part of that, she reminded herself. It didn't mean that he hadn't accepted money or gifts from his evil sibling, but he was innocent of his brother's crimes. If anyone should feel guilty, it was her, but she did not. The end justified the means. That was her new motto. She intended to use him to lure his death-dealing brother into a trap. Despite the break in the relationship with his only sibling, biology dictated a bond that assuredly went deep. He might hate what his brother did, but to plot his sibling's downfall was another concept altogether, one toward which he might very well be disinclined. The only way to most reasonably assure his cooperation was to mislead him. She'd already lied to him repeatedly and would several times more before this first meeting was over. Paul Reyes would have no fond memories of her when this was over.

"As you can see," she said as she moved through the first section of the presentation, "our gallery would display your ability to capture the essence of the sand and water and sky to its fullest advantage. Southern California isn't unlike the Keys, in more ways than perhaps you realize. Your work would fit in very nicely, would bring a fresh perspective to our gallery's already outstanding offerings. We have an international clientele, more so than you'll find here, no disrespect to the local talent or trade."

"Please," he made a sweeping motion toward the computer screen with one hand, "go on."

Renee couldn't determine if he was intrigued yet,

but she still had his full attention and that was something. As the final slide in the proposal was displayed on the screen, she made the next move. "I know you'll need some time to think over all of this. Perhaps we could have dinner tomorrow evening." She lifted one shoulder in the barest of shrugs. "Discuss any questions you might have in a more relaxed, nonbusiness rendezvous."

His hesitation was expected. As a recluse, he would have no desire to leave his sanctuary. However, the invitation needed to be standard. The average person wouldn't know all that she did about him. The slightest misstep could give away her true agenda.

"That's an excellent idea, Renee." He glanced at the computer screen one last time. "I'll review your proposal more thoroughly and make my final decision. I would prefer, however," his gaze connected with hers once more, "to have our next rendezvous here. I assume that will be acceptable to you?"

Exactly the answer she had hoped for. "Of course." Now for the finishing touch. "I'll be in town for the next few days. My schedule is completely at your disposal, Mr. Reyes."

"Paul," he suggested for the first time since her arrival.

She smiled, held his gaze a beat. "Paul." This she said with a breathy quality that caused his pupils to flare and the corners of his mouth to lift slightly. The

idea that she might be better at this than she'd antici-
pated gave her confidence a major boost.

The tension crackled ever so slightly as he blatantly assessed her for a second time, taking his slow,
sweet time. "Seven," he said, breaking the spell,
"would that work for you?"

"Seven definitely works for me." She reached for
her bag. "I look forward to discussing our future
working relationship and seeing more of your paintings." Her expression turned visibly hopeful with the
last.

"That can certainly be arranged." He placed his
hand at the small of her back as he guided her to the
hall and toward the front door. "My studio provides
a great deal of inspiration." He paused as they
reached the entry hall and looked directly at her. "At
times, however, I find myself in need of additional
stimulation. A beautiful woman can be extremely
stirring to a man's blood."

Now they were getting somewhere, it seemed. "I
can't wait to see your studio."

The smile slid back into place. "You will receive
the grand tour, I assure you."

A definite click followed by a roaring sound,
similar to that of several garage doors closing simultaneously, jerked his attention back toward the
interior of the house. Renee followed his gaze.

Barriers slowly closed down over the windows,
blocking the magnificent view. Had a hurricane

warning triggered the house's security system? The metal-on-metal action of locks being set in motion hauled her attention back to the front door.

What the hell was happening?

"Renee." Reyes swiveled to face her. "Something is wrong. You must run! Now!"

He reached for the door, but it was locked. He tugged at it frantically.

Her pulse shot into warp speed. "The security system," she urged, "can you shut it down?" Apparently the system had gone into some sort of automatic secure mode.

Reaching for the keypad next to the door he fairly shouted, "I do not understand this." He jabbed buttons to no avail. "This has never happened before."

Footfalls on the floor behind them had her wheeling around. Two men. Large. Threatening. She dropped into a crouch, her attention riveted on the two men advancing as she grabbed for her weapon.

"Don't move!" the first man barked, his weapon leveled on her.

With no desire to get killed, she pushed her hands up and slowly rose to her full height once more.

"Who are you?" Reyes demanded. "What do you want?"

"You," the second man snapped as he moved in close enough to press the barrel of his .9 millimeter against Reyes's forehead.

As Renee attempted to position herself between

the two men in an effort to protect Reyes, an arm went around her neck. Something like a mask closed over her mouth and nose. She fought the strong arms manacling her. Her lungs burning, she gasped for air.

Then her vision narrowed until there was nothing.

Her body stopped fighting and went limp.

Merida, Mexico
Same Day 6:50 p.m.

HIS EYES HAD CLOSED, the lids far too heavy to restrain. Staying awake was no longer possible. The weariness had overtaken him quickly this night. Too many sleepless ones had come and gone. He needed to rest...but if he slipped too deeply into that welcoming oblivion, he might not hear the enemy's arrival.

He needed to stay awake. Yet he was so very tired. For days that had become weeks, he had fought the temptation, had struggled to survive on stolen moments of mere dozing. He could trust no one.

How much longer could he be held prisoner this way?

What purpose did his brother hope to serve with his actions? None of this made sense. He had long ago taken leave of his brother's company. Refused to be a part of his love of spreading pain and death.

The click of the lock jerked his head up and his eyes wide open.

It could be the devil...come to finish the job at

last. Part of him would be glad to have this nightmare over. This moment had been coming for years. He should have seen that. No one would be left to bear witness to his rottenness. Escaping the reality of their strained relationship had been merely a dream. One could not deny evil when it thrived in his very blood.

The door opened slowly. Even in the near darkness, he saw the hesitant movement of his visitor. Not his brother. Some amount of relief lowered the choking tension to a more tolerable level. His eyes had days ago adjusted to the lack of light.

Juanita cautiously peeked around the partially opened door. *"Señor?"* Her voice was small and worried. She should be worried. She had played a part in this vile plan, had made herself an accomplice to his brother's selfish scheming.

In spite of the many reasons to doubt the possibility, hope stirred. Had he at last gained an ally? Or was this another trick?

"Have you had a change of heart, woman?" He asked this in English, refused to speak the native tongue of his betrayers. He had known this woman since he was a small boy. His mother had trusted her, had allowed her to look after her only children. Were his mother still alive, she would be gravely disappointed. There was no longer any loyalty in this family.

Juanita slipped into the room that had served as a prison for the past month, or had it been longer? On some level, he had reconciled to the likely fate that he would die here.

The light that followed Juanita into his prison accentuated the somber features of her thin face and her downcast gaze. He imagined that guilt kept her from looking him in the eye. He was being held prisoner in his own birth home. He had given up on the possibility of ever seeing the light of day again. His own people had turned on him, motivated by whatever threats made or gifts offered by his monster of a brother.

"I have, *señor*," Juanita confessed sadly. "You were right. He is evil. I have heard whispers that he plans to cut off your head—" she shuddered "—when he returns. No matter what you've done, I cannot allow him to harm you this way."

The threat of death was not unexpected. Why else would he be held prisoner like this? There was no turning back now. Whatever his brother was up to, he would leave no loose ends to fray. Yet even as the anger against his last living blood relative expanded inside him, he yearned for answers. His heart wouldn't simply let go of the need to know the answers as to why he had come to be in this position, at the mercy of his own kin. What had changed? Why the sudden determination to come against him…after all this time? There had to be some scheme in place.

He should have gone to the authorities years ago and put a stop to his brother's dealings. As a child, he had promised his mother that he would look out for his brother. Even then, she had known that something was not right with her eldest child. Maintaining his allegiance to that promise had been a mistake; looking the other way for so many years was a crime.

If he survived what was to come, he would settle this score once and for all.

"And what is it I have done that has brought about my imprisonment and impending death?" he asked the woman hovering with such uncertainty.

She eased back a step, positioning herself in the open doorway as if she feared she might need to quickly run away. Still, she refused to meet his gaze. "*Señor*, there is no need to speak of the past unless it is to pray for mercy on your soul."

Her hand trembled as it came to rest on the door in preparation for yanking it closed if necessary. Would she rather lock him back up in this room than answer a simple question?

"We must speak of it, Juanita," he insisted, "for I have no idea why this has happened." Other than the fact that his brother was as insane as his vile acts would suggest. But there would be much more than that. The need to uncover this plan sent much-needed adrenaline pumping through him. "Tell me what it is that you believe I have done."

For several moments, he was certain she did not intend to answer. Finally, her mouth worked mutely for a moment and then the words tumbled out. "You killed them, *señor*. All of them." Her voice trembled. She cleared her throat and began again. "Your brother put you here to protect you until he could ensure the authorities were satisfied. But I have learned that he plans to kill you himself, not protect you at all. I cannot permit such a thing. Your *madre* would not want me to allow this end, no matter your crimes."

This made no sense. He had not killed anyone. "Who have I killed, Juanita?"

"The missionaries," she whispered, then crossed herself. "You killed them all."

Shock radiated through him, rendering him momentarily unable to speak. "You are sure they are dead? All five?" His voice was quavering.

Juanita nodded jerkily. "The authorities are saying the rebels did the killing. Your brother saw to it that your name was kept from the trouble that has finally grown quiet. But now he plans to kill you so that you cannot do such a thing again. It was an act against God the Father." She crossed herself once more. "Your brother says that your death is necessary in order to obtain forgiveness for you as well as for himself." At last she lifted her gaze to his. "I have known you since you were a small boy. I cannot watch you die by the hand of your own brother. Forgiveness or no forgiveness, it is not right."

"What shall we do about this, Juanita?" He wanted to rise up from his position on the floor. To urge the woman who had known him for most of his life to act now. There was no time to waste. But he did not want to risk frightening her with any sudden moves. In addition, the price could prove to be very high if Juanita's participation in his escape were discovered before an end could be put to the enemy— his own brother.

"You must hurry back to your home in the north, *señor*," Juanita offered. "You must go now. There can be no delay. Eduardo has heard that your brother is already on his way here. He will not follow you to the north, as you well know. You must never return to Mexico. No one else can die in the Reyes' name. God will not forgive any of us, I fear."

He had not killed anyone, but Juanita was right about one thing—no one else should die in the Reyes' name, period. "How am I to go back to the States, Juanita? I have no papers. No money."

She exhaled a careworn breath. "Eduardo makes a way. Your brother's private plane waits. You must hurry. I have clothes for you."

"What will you and Eduardo do when my brother finds me gone from here?" Eduardo, Juanita's husband, had taken a great risk, as had Juanita.

She shook her head. "There is no time to talk of this. You must go."

He got up slowly. Even though she knew his intentions, Juanita gasped when he took a step toward the door.

His chest tightened at the idea that anyone would consider him threatening. That was the part of this ugly mess that he hated the most. His own brother had used him to create fear…to kill.

"Juanita," he said softly, "I have not killed anyone. If the missionaries—" his throated constricted "—are dead, then my brother or his men killed them. You surely know I would never do such a thing."

Those five men, volunteers from the Basilica de Guadalupe on the north side of Mexico City, had been working with him in a small southern village devastated by last year's floods. They had rebuilt many homes already, but there was much more to be done. Now those men were dead if what Juanita said was to be believed. What in God's name did his brother hope to prove?

"I have been thinking that you did not," Juanita admitted, her voice grave. "But I do not know the truth, *señor*. Flee this place. If your heart is pure you will flourish again."

If only it were that easy. "I understand." His brother could be charming and utterly persuasive when he chose. No one wanted to believe the depth of his depravity.

"You must hurry, *mi hijo*."

"Thank you, Juanita."

Their gazes met briefly in the near darkness. Years had passed since she had last used that endearment. If they survived, he would ensure that her attempt to do the right thing was well compensated. Of the handful who knew of this despicable arrangement, no one else had dared to offer a hand in support. Those who had looked the other way would not be forgotten, either.

He followed Juanita from the prison. His breath sawed in and out of his lungs despite his attempt to stay calm and steady. If they were caught, Juanita would die. His own fate might very well be no better, though most would not dare attempt to use lethal force to stop him for fear of his brother's reprisal. In any event, what did he have to lose? His fate had already been decided by his brother. A sharp pain pierced his chest at the thought of those men who had lost their lives already. Innocent men who had done nothing more than attempt to help those less fortunate.

His brother would pay this time.

Fury bolted through him. For the first time in his life, he felt certain he could do what needed to be done, putting aside that long-ago promise once and for all.

It was time for his brother's reign of terror to end.

Chapter Three

Renee woke with a start. She frowned, feeling groggy. She swallowed, licked her lips. Her mouth was dry, tasted bitter. A strange odor lingered in her lungs, making her gasp for more air.

Where the hell was she?

She rolled onto her side, only then realizing that she lay on the cold tile floor. A shiver quaked through her. Damn, she was cold. Struggling up to a sitting position, she surveyed the room. It was nearly dark, the space lit by a single lamp in one corner.

A brown couch, two stripped chairs and a single oak table with a lamp. A den, maybe? But there was no television or game tables of any sort. No windows and just one door.

The image of a man subduing Paul Reyes flickered to the forefront of her hazy thoughts.

She scrambled to her feet and rushed to the door. She braced against it and twisted the knob.

Locked.

Renee looked around again as she slumped against the wall. Whatever inhalant they had used to put her out still had her equilibrium off-kilter. Her reasoning was fragmented. Her balance out of whack. *Wear it off.* She pushed away from the wall and walked around the room, slow and steady at first. Moving around would help her body metabolize the remnants of the drug. She wished for water. It was ironic that a whole ocean of water sat right outside while she was thirsty.

Evidently, one of the men had taken Paul Reyes and the other had locked her in here. Had they killed him? Were they Victor's men? Was Victor here?

She had to get out of this room.

The longer she walked, the clearer her mind became. She couldn't be sure how much time had passed. There was every reason to believe that she was in the basement since there were no windows. She went back to the door and gave it a couple of kicks and a few body slams. The door wasn't budging. She moved on to the wall next to the door that separated this room from the next. Smooth, painted. Not concrete or cinder block, which was good. It looked and felt like drywall. If that was the case, then it would be about half an inch thick, attached to either steel or wood two-by-fours installed at a set distance apart. She wasn't sure of the exact distance, but figured at least twelve inches.

Only one way to find out.

She needed more light. After unplugging the lamp, she moved to that same wall and plugged the lamp in the nearest socket. Then she discarded the shade so that the full force of the light would be available. Shining the light slowly over the wall, she searched for imperfections. Any indication of the nail or screw line to confirm her assumption. A smile nudged her lips as she found what she was looking for. She set the lamp aside and started knocking on the wall until she felt certain she had found a space between the two-by-fours.

Then she turned, facing away from the wall and kicked backwards, pounding her foot into the drywall as hard as she could, about eighteen inches above the floor. She kicked hard. If there was anyone close by, they would come running soon.

She repeated the process again and again. The slight give her action produced assured her that she had guessed right about this particular interior wall being composed of drywall.

Her leg started to give out so she shifted her position and used the other one, again putting all the force she possessed behind the effort. After a few more well-placed kicks, she got what she wanted: a hole. From there she pulled and tugged, breaking away the drywall and revealing steel studs. That left the layer of drywall on the other side of the studs the only barrier between her and escape. An electrical wire that likely linked the sockets in that room snaked through the studs about a foot off the floor. The wire's presence wouldn't be a problem. All she had to do was be sure she kicked above it as she'd done before.

Thankfully, no one showed up to stop her.

Maybe it was her imagination, but the process went a little more quickly this time. Before long, she had herself a hole about four feet high and around twelve or fourteen inches wide. Careful of the wire, she wiggled out between the studs.

For the first time, she had reason to appreciate the fact that her brother had put his fist through her living room wall once. Otherwise she might not have thought of this. At least he'd been good for something.

On the other side was what seemed like a corridor. It was too narrow to be a room, but there was no light at all for her to have visual confirmation. She dusted herself off and felt her way along the wall. She encountered another door, opened it and flipped the light switch. An overhead light came on, illuminating the space to reveal a bedroom. A telephone on the bedside table had her rushing over to it. Dead. She dropped the receiver and moved back into the corridor.

The direction in which she'd been headed was a

dead end, so she turned around and went the other way. She opened two more doors, one lead to what appeared to be a storeroom cluttered with leftover pieces of furniture and boxes of discarded clothing. The other door led to another bedroom. Again, the phone was dead.

At this end of the corridor was a staircase. She took a couple of deep steadying breaths before she started upward. The electricity was on, but so far the phones were dead. When she'd come into this house, the sky had been clear. She didn't remember hearing about any bad weather headed this way, so the dead phone lines were more likely related to the two intruders who had shown up and locked her down here.

Though no one had come running while she kicked through the wall, that didn't mean she was alone in the house. Her senses on high alert, she took the final steps up and moved into the kitchen, braced for most anything. The hurricane shutters were still locked in place, shielding the view through the windows. The metal shutters would be pretty much impenetrable, eliminating the windows as an exit. Since she didn't know the deactivation code for the security system, there was no way to disarm it.

As she moved through the ground floor, a lamp here and there provided enough illumination to discourage her from switching on additional lighting. The shadows provided by the dim lighting might prove beneficial.

Her heart pounded hard against her sternum as she progressed from room to room, checking phone lines and looking for anything useful. The computer had been disabled, the monitor smashed and wires cut at the back of the hard drive, rendering the system worthless. She found her purse on the floor near the front door where she'd dropped it. Her cell phone and gun were gone. They'd taken her ankle holster as well, she realized abruptly. So far she hadn't found any bodies, dead or alive, in any of the rooms she'd checked.

The front door was locked. She considered the keypad next to it. Red lights blared at her, warning that the system remained fully armed. If she unlocked and opened the door, the alarm would go off and the police would come. At least that was the way it worked under normal circumstances.

Might as well give it a try. There was nothing else she could do here. Maintaining her cover didn't appear necessary at this point. Paul Reyes was long gone...or dead.

She turned the lock button, then gripped the knob, gave it a twist and...nothing. She twisted the latch built into the knob again. This time, the knob turned, but the door didn't budge.

Frustration sent a prick of panic along her nerve endings. She wiped her sweaty palms on her slacks and reached to try again. Her gaze settled on the dead bolt. No wonder it wouldn't open. She'd forgotten to unlock the dead bolt.

Apparently her brain was still suffering the after-effects of the drug or she would have noticed that sooner. Exhaling a ragged breath, she started to reach up, then realized that this was the kind of dead bolt that required a key for locking and unlocking it. No turn piece on the dead bolt.

"Damn."

Don't panic, she reminded herself. Find another door. She turned around to retrace her steps. Why would those scumbags just leave her here? Why not kill her and dispose of her body? Where was Paul? If he was dead, where was his body?

Her heart started to thump hard again. Had Victor taken his brother from her reach? Had he somehow known why she was here? That seemed unlikely.

She hesitated at the bottom of the stairs. Before she did anything else, she had to be sure he wasn't up there. Her gaze followed the elegant staircase as it wound upward to the next floor. She couldn't imagine why he would have been taken upstairs and then murdered, but then murder didn't always make sense.

He wasn't in the basement or anywhere on the first floor. If the upper floor was clear, then she would know for certain he'd been taken from the house. Dead or alive. She placed her hand on the cool metal banister. Get this part over with.

Listening intently, she climbed the stairs. The upstairs corridor went left and right. The walls were richly paneled in a natural wood that glowed like warm honey. The floor was carpeted, muffling the sound of her footsteps. She went right first. Three bedrooms, each with its own bath. All with dead phones. No bodies. No usable weapons.

At the other end of the corridor was a single set of double doors. The master bedroom suite, she presumed. She opened the doors and turned on the overhead light. Two chandeliers twinkled, spilling a brilliant glow over the room. Same rich paneling as in the hall. The wall nearest the door offered floor-to-ceiling shelves lined with books and lovely objects the owner had collected. A big king-sized bed sat against the opposite wall. Several windows adorned with lavish curtains. Still, no blood, no body. The telephone was out of commission, just like all the others.

There was a massive walk-in closet and lots of fancy suits. A wall safe and dozens of pairs of shoes. Jewelry. A person could have set up an entire men's department with what was in that one closet.

Seemed like a hell of a large wardrobe and bling for a recluse.

The master bath epitomized the term *luxurious*. No working phone, no body. Nothing appeared out of place.

What the hell was going on?

It wasn't until she'd got halfway across the bed-room headed for the door that she noticed what looked like a painting on the wall was actually a framed plasma television. Using the remote, she turned it on, mainly to see if it worked and to check any possible alerts that might explain part of what had happened. A news channel bloomed to life on the wide screen. The sound was muted but the crawler revealed no weather alerts. She started to power it off when she noticed the Security button on the remote. She pressed it. The channel instantly went to a multi-view screen that displayed various exterior locations around the property. The front door, back door, garage entry as well as the dock, the driveway and an overall rear property panorama.

It was dark outside. The security screen showed the time as 1:15 a.m. She'd been out for hours. Her car and the Maserati were still parked exactly where they had been on the front parking patio.

This was nuts.

She tossed the remote back onto the bed and turned to go, but stopped dead in her tracks.

Her gaze collided with dark eyes...eyes she'd seen before.

Paul?

She searched the grim face...noted the day's growth of beard. She didn't remember that.

He wasn't wearing the same clothes he'd worn when she arrived.

Victor?

Her heart rammed against her sternum. She

couldn't be sure. The urge to flee exploded inside her, but before she could put thought into action he spoke.

"Who are you?"

She blinked, confusion defusing her fear.

"Why are you here?" he demanded in that same silky voice she'd found so pleasant only a few hours ago.

Could this be the same man?

"I'm—"

He held up a hand to silence her, his gaze suddenly riveted to the television screen. She turned her head just far enough to look there as well. The air evaporated in her lungs.

Men dressed in black fatigues and armed to the teeth were crawling all over the property. Police? Two men were at the front door preparing to knock it down with a battering ram.

A hand clamped around her right arm. Her attention snapped back to the man now standing next to her.

"If you want to live, you'll do exactly as I say," he said sharply, his fingers tightening with each word.

"That's the police," she bluffed. "I called them." She would have but the phones were dead. But her bluff might work.

One beat, two. "No," he countered. "You didn't call anyone."

It didn't matter, she realized, whether this was Paul or Victor. It appeared to be bad either way. She lifted her chin in defiance of the trembling that had started in her limbs. "They'll bust in here looking for me. But I suppose that's a risk you'll have to take." More bluffing, but it could work.

Mentally measuring his callused grip on her arm and the distance to the door, she considered how far she would get before he caught her.

"Those men are not here to rescue you," he said flatly. "You can come with me or we will both die."

Renee glanced at the monitor. She could hear the ramming against the front door as she watched the action playing out on the screen like a cop flick. The men would be inside in seconds. They looked official. Could she trust that assumption? She turned back to the man still clutching her arm. If he was Paul Reyes, she needed him to bait his brother. If he was Victor, then she had accomplished her mission. All she had to do was survive long enough to let Gates get his hands on him.

Right now, her best option was to go along with him. She needed him—at least for a little while longer.

"Where are we going?"

"This way."

He ushered her to the far side of the bedroom to the wall lined with bookshelves that likely separated this room from the next. He touched something on the underside of one of the lower shelves and a section of wall opened outward. As she stood there gaping, he grabbed her arm and ushered her inside the secret room. The breakaway wall closed and what she concluded were hidden locks clicked into place.

The lighting was dim, but she could see quite well. A cot sat against one wall. Shelves filled with supplies of all kinds, including food and water, were stacked in the back section of the room. Three small monitors blinked to life, each one displaying a different area in the house or the property outside.

"What is this place?" she whispered.

"You don't have to whisper," he said. "The room is soundproof."

A panic room, she realized after closer inspection. She'd heard of these. There was probably a telephone in here. One that had a separate line, just like the electricity. That was the whole point of one of these rooms. A person could hide in safety, and nothing done anywhere else in the house would affect the protected environment. She covertly glanced around. The phone was probably stowed behind supplies or built into the monitoring system. The movement on the screens distracted her. A dozen or more men were prowling through the house. In here she couldn't hear a sound as they shuffled from room to room in those heavy black boots.

Who were these guys? As if one of the men shown

on monitor two had heard her question, he turned away from the camera. Large, block style white letters were emblazoned across his back:

D...E...A.

Adrenaline surged. One of those men could be Gates. She held herself still, risked a look at the man standing a few feet away. If he was Victor Reyes, this could be the moment she'd come here to make happen.

As if she'd somehow telegraphed the thought, he turned his head and stared straight into her eyes.

"Who are you?"

His question startled her, but she suppressed any outward expression. "Don't you know?" Could this be Paul Reyes? She'd met Paul, had gone over the proposed gallery contract with him. He had been observant, infinitely charming and confident, with a calm but forceful manner. However, this man seemed agitated, uncertain, harsh even. His lean frame was all muscle...his hands were not smooth and soft as Paul's had been. Now that she studied him more closely, the stubble on his face was no mere day's growth...more like three or four.

"Who are *you?*" she demanded, turning the question back on him. Her breathing slowed just a little as her ability to reason overrode her initial trepidation. Surely if he had intended to kill her, he would have done that already. She was relatively certain at this point that he was not armed. The confusion he radiated was the one element that gave her pause.

"Answer the question," he ordered, his tone gruff.

"Renee Parsons," she lied, sticking with her cover for all the good it would do. "I represent a gallery in L.A." She amplified the indignation in her expression, as well as her tone, just to make sure that he knew she was not happy. "I came all this way to work out a deal to show the paintings of Paul Reyes in our gallery. What the hell is going on here? Who are you?"

For several seconds he didn't respond. If this was Victor Reyes, as she suspected, did he not know the truth about who she was? Could she be that lucky? When had he arrived? Then again, if he wasn't aware of her true business here, why had he shown up? Stepping onto American soil was a death sentence. Killing a cop was a capital offense. He was certainly aware of the risk he had taken making this personal appearance. Why not simply walk into his brother's home and do whatever he'd come here to do? Why the game? And if this was Victor, where was Paul?

Her breath caught when two of the agents entered the master bedroom and looked around. Every instinct urged her to scream at the top of her lungs, maybe pound on the wall that separated the panic room from where the men stood. But he had said this room was soundproof. If she took that risk and it didn't pan out, she would have accomplished nothing more than making this man angry with her. It was bad enough that she was trapped in here with him; she didn't need him ticked off.

"I do not understand."

His comment dragged her attention back to him. Bewildered, she said quite frankly, "Well, you're not in that boat alone." He had to be playing her. Whatever his hidden agenda, she wasn't going to let him trap her into saying or doing anything that would get her into more trouble than she was already in.

The men methodically tearing apart the house belonging to Paul Reyes captured her attention once more. What were they looking for? The two who had scanned the bedroom moved on to another room.

She turned to her host—or abductor. "What if they find us? Aren't you worried?"

He watched the monitors for half a minute. "They won't find us. This room is undetectable."

Her focus settled on the monitors once more. "I'd hate to be you if you're wrong."

Silence thickened for several minutes. She folded her arms over her chest and pretended to be unaffected by her present circumstances. She had no idea what this man had planned, but she would be damned if she would allow him to see just how terrified she was. She hated admitting that to herself, but she was pretty damned scared.

He turned around. She gasped, then cursed herself when he assessed her at length. Without commenting, he crossed to the shelves and removed two pouches of water. He offered one to her.

She started to decline, but that bad taste still

lingered in her mouth and her throat was cotton dry. She accepted the pouch and followed the instructions for opening it. Though the water was room temperature, it felt good against her throat.

For several minutes, he continued to watch this defacing of the home without comment or outward reaction. Her curiosity swiftly got the better of her.

"Where is Paul?" she asked, deciding that she might as well get him talking again. Once these guys found whatever they were looking for or decided to call it quits, she would be left alone with this guy. Maybe not a good scenario.

"My brother was in this house with you?" he countered.

Was he hedging? Avoiding her question? "Yes, your brother was here with me." As if she would have been in the house alone. "The two gorillas who showed up last night took him." She really couldn't say for sure they did, but that was the only conclusion she could reach. "They locked me in a room in the basement."

His brow lined as if he were working hard to make sense of what she had told him. "These men, what did they look like?"

This was getting stranger by the moment. If this guy wasn't the man she was with last night, and clearly he wasn't, then he had to be Victor. Why would Victor be standing here asking her these questions? Why the hell would he be here, period, unless he'd gotten wind of her true agenda? That was unlikely since she'd only gotten here an hour before trouble had shown up. Surely a man who hid out in Mexico couldn't have acted that quickly.

Since her response was necessary for the conversation to resume, she shrugged. "Big, muscled-up guys. Both wore black." She nodded to the monitors. "Not like these guys, not uniforms, just casual civilian clothes."

"My brother did not know these men?"

How did she get this across to him? "He told me to run. One of the guys stuck a gun to his head. I'm pretty sure if he knew them, he didn't like them very much."

More silence.

He moved closer to the monitors and studied the goings-on. "This is wrong."

Did he think that he could fool her into believing he was Paul by acting as if none of this made sense to him? Not going to happen.

He turned to her as if he'd sensed her conclusion. His timing was eerie.

"I am Paul Reyes. This is my home. The man you met last night was probably my brother Victor. These men—" he gestured to the monitors "—must be looking for him."

"I'll need proof," she challenged. As it stood, she had absolutely no reason to believe him. The whole situation was out of hand. Whatever his game, she wasn't playing along. "I saw Paul's work, spoke with the gallery owner. She spoke highly of how well Paul handled his last show. She—"

"Mallory Rogers?" he interrupted. "Ms. Rogers has a discriminating eye for art, that much is true, but we have never met."

Renee felt her gaze narrow, but she kept her immediate response of "yeah, right" to herself. "Ms. Rogers seemed to know Paul quite well." In fact, Renee got the distinct impression the two had a connection of sorts.

The man now claiming to be Paul Reyes shook his head. "Impossible. We have never met."

Strange. He sounded completely sincere and yet he had to be lying. He couldn't be telling the truth. Other than the fact that the two men could pass for twins, this guy was nothing like the man she'd met last night. The button-down shirt he wore was plain, a faded blue, the material distressed cotton. Well-worn jeans and sneakers. His black hair looked shaggy, as if he needed a trim. No. This was wrong, somehow. He couldn't be Paul Reyes, the refined artist who lived in this extravagant house.

"Why would your brother pretend to be you?" That was the real question. She could be open-minded as long as the facts backed up the conclusion. If the man who had represented himself to her as Paul was, in fact, Victor, what was his motivation? Why would a ruthless drug lord come to Key Largo and pretend to be someone he wasn't? Victor's M.O. usually included killing anyone in his way, not masquerading as that person. She was certain if the man with whom she'd chatted last night had been Victor Reyes and he had wanted her dead, she would be dead. Not to mention the risk he would have taken coming here. What would have been his ultimate goal? He'd have to be pretty damned motivated to come here, considering he was on DEA's wanted list.

Her mystery man didn't answer right away, then he said, "My brother and I have not spoken in years."

"Your brother doesn't appreciate the business you do?" she suggested, recognizing the risk that she might inflame his fury but willing to take it. Every good prosecutor knew how to lead a witness. Someone was lying to her, the man last night or this new guy. If not for the stubble that couldn't be faked, she would even go so far as to believe they were one in the same.

His gaze remained steady on the monitors. "My brother refuses to acknowledge the passion I feel for our people. Or—" he glanced at her then "—for my work."

She had to hand it to him, he had his story and he was sticking to it.

"I don't know why he would lure you here under false pretenses," he went on, the lines on his face deepening with something like regret. "Or why he would assume my life. But I am quite positive that it is not for good."

Ah, so he wanted her to believe that the man she'd met last night had stolen his identity. The idea wasn't impossible, she supposed, but where was his proof? "Can you prove that you're Paul Reyes?" Even as she asked the question she mentally acknowledged a cold hard fact. She couldn't say that he wasn't Paul based on the photos she'd seen. Neither Paul nor Victor had ever been arrested, which meant no fingerprints. Damn. There was something no one had given any real consideration. She'd come here assuming the man who lived in this house was Paul Reyes. Unless one or both had distinguishing physical marks not readily visible, making a conclusive identification might be next to impossible. There had been nothing in the file about any particular marks that might set one man apart from the other.

But why would his brother pretend to be him? The DEA wanted Victor fiercely. Surely he would not be so arrogant as to believe that no one would notice that he'd taken his brother's place. Again, she was back to the idea of motivation. What compelling reason did Victor Reyes have to do this?

"I cannot prove anything at the moment."

Therein lay the rub.

"Then how can you expect me to believe you?" And where did that leave her?

The man who might or might not be Victor Reyes

turned to look her in the eyes. "For the same reason I believe you are Renee Parsons."

Well, he had her there. And, unknowingly, he had just proven her point.

"You said this was your name," he continued. "I have no reason to believe otherwise."

Aha! "But I do have reason to believe otherwise about you," she argued. "I've already met Paul Reyes. Why would the other man have lied?"

That dark gaze probed deeper than was comfortable, but she held her ground. "I cannot answer that question. I can unconditionally say, however, that whatever Victor's plans, he must be stopped."

For the first time since he'd grabbed her by the arm and ushered her into this hidden room, she considered that this whole thing could be some sort of elaborate hoax. For what end? In her experience, men like Victor Reyes didn't go off half-cocked. He planned. He manipulated. He succeeded. There would be no glitches.

This was a definite glitch.

"If the man I met last night was Victor," she offered, "and if he has, for some as yet unknown reason, assumed your identity here in Florida, where have you been? Why were you not aware of his activities?" She gave herself a mental pat on the back for coming up with a perfectly logical question to which he would have difficulty professing he didn't know the answer.

"I was working in a village in Oaxaca." At her puzzled expression, he clarified. "Oaxaca is a state in southern Mexico where there is much poverty." He sighed, the sound grievous as if even the thought of the place disturbed him. "Many of the strong, young men who grew up there have escaped to the United States to work in the fields and vineyards since there is no real money to be made at home. Only the women and elderly are left behind. Last year's floods brought much hardship, and there was no one to look to for help."

Renee thought of his callused palms. "You were helping rebuild the village?" She could believe that, but his work there had nothing to do with here and now.

"I was one among many."

He looked tired. She stared at his hands when he shoved his fingers through his hair as if he needed to clear his head of the burden straining his thoughts. The image made her wonder how an artist could take such risks with the hands that created his beloved art. Wasn't he afraid of injuring himself?

Wait. That was assuming he was Paul Reyes and she wasn't ready to make that assumption just yet. She needed more concrete evidence.

"So you were away helping with the rebuilding and your brother stole your life?" Hadn't she seen a movie with that same story line? It wasn't that the idea was implausible; it just seemed awfully convenient at the moment. Everything she had on Paul Reyes indicated he rarely left his home. Working as a volunteer among strangers didn't fit with his usual M.O.

"Yes."

"You have witnesses who can confirm you were there and who will uphold your assertion that you are Paul Reyes the artist?"

He inclined his head, searched her eyes, his lacking some of the intensity she had noticed before, the change insinuating he had come to some sort of realization. "Perhaps. I cannot say for sure." His expression went blank as if he feared giving away too much. Then he said, "You do not speak like an art buyer, Ms. Parsons."

"How would you know?" she shot right back. "You've never met one…have you?" He'd insisted that he'd never met Mallory Rogers, the gallery owner in Key Largo. If that was true, there was every likelihood that he had not met anyone else in the business. At least not more than once, and then most likely only in the briefest of encounters.

He smiled. The unexpected act caught her totally off guard. That single action entirely changed the way he looked; even his posture relaxed visibly. Gone was the intimidating harshness, replaced by an undeniable gentleness that seemed far more natural.

"You are correct, Ms. Parsons, I have not."

"Renee."

His questioning look made her want to bite off her tongue. Maybe that was too fast. Don't second-guess, she reminded herself. But she didn't let him see the way she faltered. She had a mission. Lure Victor Reyes into a trap. If this man was Paul Reyes, she needed his cooperation. If he was Victor Reyes, she needed only to prove it...somehow.

"You can call me Renee."

"Renee," he parroted.

"You say someone in the village where you volunteered might be able to confirm your identity?" she ventured, since they were on such good terms now.

The last remnants of the smile she'd appreciated disappeared, replaced by what looked like sadness.

"Some have died."

She blinked, refused to be taken in by those dark, soulful eyes. He could be lying to her, probably was. "I still don't see the motivation for why your brother would want to pretend to be you." If she kept coming at him with that same question, eventually she'd get a real answer, or at least a different one.

His expression closed completely. "I told you. I have no idea." He turned his attention back to the monitors.

She supposed that helping to rebuild a village would give a man that weary, weathered look. He could be telling the truth about that part. But the rest of his story was just too circumstantial—not to mention that the timing was way coincidental. "What brought you back now? How did you hear about what your brother was up to?" If he'd been in southern Mexico, who had made him aware of his brother's activities?

He didn't shift his attention from the monitors. "One month ago, I unexpectedly returned to our childhood home in Merida to secure additional manpower. My brother's men imprisoned me there. I was held against my will until last night. I had no idea why."

The DEA guys appeared to be winding down their search. Her pulse quickened at the idea that they would leave soon and she would be here alone with whoever the hell this guy was. She settled her gaze on Reyes. "How did you get away?" Follow the logic, find the faults in his responses and she would find the lies and hopefully part of the truth.

"A member of the household staff finally recognized my helplessness in my brother's schemes and arranged for my escape. I did not ask why the sudden change of heart. I was anxious to get away."

"So there is a household staff who can confirm your identity?"

His gaze collided with hers. "If any of them are still alive, yes."

Her gaze narrowed. "Why would your brother kill them?"

"For the same reason he will kill me or anyone else who gets in his way."

Movement on one of the monitors jerked both their gazes back there. Four of the men had returned to the master bedroom. Each picked a different section of the room and started a new search. One zeroed in on the bookshelves.

Reyes tensed.

Renee looked from him to the monitor and back. "Are they going to find us?" She wasn't so sure that was entirely a bad thing...but she needed to be sure who this man was before anything else happened or anyone, even the DEA, interfered.

"If they do—" those dark eyes connected with hers once more "—then my brother will have won."

Chapter Four

Chicago
Thursday, May 3, 3:00 a.m.

Jim heaved a breath and scrubbed the sleep from his burning eyes. He'd fallen asleep at his desk waiting for a call from Vaughn. She still wasn't answering her cell phone. He hadn't heard from her since the morning before. Almost twenty-four hours had passed. Something was definitely wrong.

A light rap on the door to his office snapped his attention upward. Who the hell would be here at this time of the morning? He was confident he'd locked both the front and rear entrances.

"I decided if you weren't coming home, I'd have to come to the office."

He smiled. Tasha, the chain holding her key to his office twirling around her finger. "What about Jamie?"

"Our daughter spent the night with her grand-mother."

Tasha, his wife of just over two years, entered the room and sat down on the edge of his desk, tossed her keys aside. His gaze slid from the length of toned legs revealed by the short black skirt to the flash of cleavage allowed by the devil-red blouse. Tension rippled through his muscles, some more than others.

"The time got away from me," he offered as his gaze swept over the woman he loved more than life itself. How strange it felt to love someone that much. He hadn't realized just how much he loved her until he'd held their daughter in his arms. He'd never felt anything quite like that. "I fell asleep. Just woke up." She looked damn good for it to be so early in the morning.

"Victoria is worried about you," she said as she slipped off one high-heeled shoe and then the other before scooting more fully onto the desktop.

His mother, Victoria Colby-Camp, worried about him too much. But, as a new father, he'd learned that worry came with the territory. He could no longer say he didn't understand.

"She always worries." He licked his lips as his gaze raked his lovely wife once more. "You'd think she would be too busy to worry about me. The new Colby Agency building is under way. Between that and running the business out of a temporary location, she should have her hands full."

"You know your mother better than that." This time when Tasha moved, she slid around to his side of the desk, pushing files and papers aside as she went. She sat with one bare foot on either side of him, spreading her legs and causing the skirt she wore to slide to the very tops of her shapely thighs. "It'll take a hell of a lot more than someone blowing up her building to distract her from what she loves most."

He grunted, too focused on devouring his wife with his eyes to form any words.

"FYI, Mr. Colby, I worry, too." She started to unbutton her blouse. "I get really worried when you don't come home at night." The last button released from its closure and she shouldered out of the silky blouse, leaving only a lacy black bra behind. "But mostly," she added as she pulled his chair closer with her feet, the rollers sliding easily on the hardwood, "I just miss my husband."

He didn't bother explaining that he could remedy that problem. He kissed her instead, kissed her long and deep. Then he pushed out of his chair and leaned her back on his desk, clearing a path as he went. The rest of his staff wouldn't be arriving for hours. There was time.

He made love to her right there. She needed him. Everything else would have to wait.

Chapter Five

Key Largo
4:00 a.m.

The four men had torn the bedroom apart in their search, evidently hadn't found what they were looking for, and left. Paul Reyes allowed himself to relax when the team designated as DEA had gone.

He had to wonder if this exercise had been for looks. To make it appear as if an investigation were under way. But what did this have to do with him?

The house had been quiet for almost one hour. His guest had stopped asking questions. Her silence proved to be as disconcerting as her tedious interrogation. She sat on the cot, her arms folded over her chest as if she felt the need to protect herself from him. He posed no harm to her, but telling her so might be premature. Assuming she preferred her distance, he leaned against the wall rather than joining her on the cot. As tired as he was, he could not let his guard down completely.

He was not sure how she fit into this perplexing scenario, but her presence could not be happenstance. Perhaps he should pursue his own line of questions. The immediate danger had passed for now. There might not be time later. If she was an enemy who represented a threat to him, he needed to know. The possibility that she was working with his brother could not be overlooked.

"How long have you lived in L.A.?" He started with the basics. Lies were most often discovered through the most elementary venues.

"Three years," she said automatically.

No delay in her response. Perhaps this answer was true. Or practiced.

"Yet you have not lost your southern accent." He was quite confident she had not lived her entire life in L.A. The west coast ability to sound "culturally anonymous" was missing. Hers was not such a thick drawl, more soft and slow…sweet, even when she was frightened or angry. An inflection pleasing to the ears.

"I made it a point not to. We're quite prideful in Georgia."

She was lying, at least in part. He had recognized those same indicators when she had told him her name. The telltale signs played out on her face, with a widening of the eyes as she glanced away and a compressing of the lips. He was not sure if her presence was relevant to what his brother was up to, but he would know in time. Patience, he had concluded, was the best route for reaching this woman. The task would not be a hardship. She was a beautiful woman. Dark hair and golden eyes. The pale creamy slacks and blouse she wore clung nicely to her womanly figure. And she was aggressive. Aggressive and intelligent. An exciting combination if their state of affairs were of a different nature.

She stood and settled that bold gaze on his. "Is there any reason why you can't just let me go now? Those men are long gone. I'd like to get out of here. This isn't exactly how I planned this trip to the Sunshine State."

Strange that she would ask this question now, seemingly out of the blue. Her sudden turnabout further roused his suspicions.

"There is only one reason," he said in answer to her question.

She waited for him to go on, her expression carefully restrained.

"You were with my brother yesterday. I must know the true reason for your visit." He steeled for her reaction. "Until I know what Victor is really up to, I cannot allow you out of my sight." She started to argue, but he stopped her with an upraised palm. "For whatever reason, you are a part of this. I must know that reason."

"He couldn't have known I was coming to see him," she protested. "I came unannounced. Used the local gallery as an opportunity to get past the gate."

This was the truth, or what she perceived to be the truth. He felt certain of that, but the response did not answer his question.

"But something happened during your visit," he maintained. "An event that coincided with my sudden release. Can you think what that might be?" He had been held prisoner for nearly one month. Juanita's explanation for his abrupt release no longer held any merit. Those DEA agents had shown up within a half hour of his arrival here. That was no coincidence. He might not have the experience of his brother in such matters, but he was no fool. He had walked into a setup gone wrong.

"No. Of course not." She looked away and stared at the floor, then at the static images on the monitors.

She was lying again. This disturbed him greatly, even as he understood that his reaction to her decision to lie was irrational. He had no reason to expect the truth from this woman. Unfortunately, there was a part of him that never ceased to expect the best from all. He should have learned better long ago.

"We should rest while we have the opportunity," he suggested, seeing no point in pursuing the issue just now. Fatigue pulled at him, clouded his ability to concentrate and form proper conclusions. Perhaps she would grow agitated and start to talk a bit more openly.

Her gaze snapped back to his as if his decision to put the matter aside for now had prompted her determination to do precisely the opposite. "Shouldn't we be trying to find your brother? How do we know he's even still alive? He might be injured and need help."

"My brother has never needed anyone in his life," he said with far more disdain than he'd intended. He modulated his emotions and, a great deal more calmly, said, "If we proceed without rest, then we are doomed to failure."

He knew this firsthand. He hadn't slept more than a few hours in days. The exhaustion clawed mercilessly at him. She was surely tired, as well. The longer he kept her to himself, the more likely he could wear down her defenses. He needed to know who she was and why she had appeared at his home. He had no worries about his brother's health. It was his, and perhaps hers, that was in danger. What he needed more than anything was her full cooperation. Isolation would work in his favor. He had never in his life taken a person hostage, but perhaps that was what this was. He needed her with him, no matter what she wanted or needed. Was that not the same thing as kidnapping?

"You need not worry about my brother," he said finally. "Unfortunately, he is far too hard to kill to have surrendered so easily. Things are not as they appear, I assure you."

She stared at him defiantly. "There are people who will be worried about me. I need a phone."

"There will be no phone calls now." At the fury that

lit in her eyes, he added, "If you do not cause me trouble, perhaps I will allow you to use the phone later." After I know your true agenda, he qualified silently.

Resigned to his decision, she plopped back down on the cot and curled her legs beneath her. She leaned against the wall and closed her eyes. If she went to sleep, perhaps he would be able to rest his eyes, as well. He was very tired. He needed to reason out what this latest turn of events meant.

He settled onto the floor and leaned his head against the wall. First his brother kills a handful of innocent missionaries, then he imprisons him in the family home. How could the dedicated people who had worked for their parents have believed anything that they were told by a man as cruel and demented as Victor?

Paul had assumed that fear had kept those who knew him from coming to his aid. Juanita and her husband, the housekeepers, and George, the gardener and groundskeeper, all three knew him…knew he was not capable of such violence. But perhaps it was not fear. Had his brother promised them money? Protection? The three were quite old now. Perhaps fear for their futures had driven them. He simply did not know.

What he did know was what he saw with his own eyes. His home here in Key Largo had been taken over by his brother. Signs of Victor were everywhere. The lavish car. New extravagant furnishings. All of it was in excess. Paul scarcely recognized his own home, so much had changed. How long had his evil sibling been pretending to be him? Months, at least.

Something had precipitated this move. Something with far-reaching implications. Had the new president of Mexico decided to consider the extradition petition the United States had made for Victor Reyes? Whatever the reason, his brother obviously wanted or needed his freedom from the ugly past that dogged his every step. The only way to achieve that was to slough off all aspects of his former self. The authorities would not be satisfied without indisputable proof that Victor Reyes was gone for good.

Paul was certain that was why those agents were searching his home. They had come expecting to find him. He would have been arrested as the venomous drug lord Victor Reyes, tried and possibly executed. Victor would have been free to assume Paul's life, a crime-free life. That had to be what this was about.

Such a good plan. Perhaps it might have even worked for a short time. But he knew Victor. He was a devil. He would never have been satisfied leading a normal, quiet life. He would have ended up ruining this life just as he had his own.

Paul had spent many years living in his brother's shadow. As children, his older brother had always been the one in charge. As an adult he was the one to make headlines while Paul lived quietly, happy with nothing more than his work. He'd kept himself so apart from the world, there was no one here who could vouch for his identity. Only Juanita, Eduardo, and George, back in Merida.

Victor would kill them, too. That was how he would retire them. Yet they foolishly trusted him.

Somehow Paul's leaving home so many months ago to devote himself to helping those less fortunate than him had provided the opportunity his brother needed. It had been years since Paul had even visited Mexico. But news of the horrendous problems in Oaxaca had propelled him to help his people. No matter that he had lived in the United States for more than a decade—Mexico was still his country, the residents there still his people.

He should have come home to check on things in Key Largo periodically. He should not have assumed that a mere caretaker would be able to protect his home or warn him in time in the event of trouble.

The thought speared through Paul's chest. Where was the caretaker? Had Victor fired him while pretending to be Paul, or had he killed him? Regret for his many mistakes tore at Paul. He should have been watching. He should have never believed that his brother would simply let him be. That had never been Victor's way.

Now, Paul had only one choice. Face Victor and end this once and for all.

That would not be such an easy feat, considering Victor had many ruthless men at his disposal.

Paul had no one. Not a single living being who

could help him. He looked at the woman who had fallen asleep. Except perhaps her. She was here for a reason that involved his brother. He was sure of it. Many people had attempted to take down his brother by using Paul for access. Was that her reason for being here? If so, he might be able to use that to his advantage. But it was unclear as yet whether she was friend or foe.

It was entirely possible that Victor had left her here to finish him off.

6:30 a.m.

THE NIGHTMARE woke Renee from her sleep.

She blinked, rubbed at her eyes and struggled to get her bearings.

Panic room…with one of the Reyes brothers.

She settled her attention on the man who leaned against the wall, his eyes closed. Whether or not he was asleep, she couldn't say. He hadn't moved since the last time she had awakened and taken notice of him sitting on the floor.

Closing her eyes, she tried to banish the lingering images from the nightmare.

He had been strapped to a shiny steel gurney, two IV lines running into his arm. She'd been watching through a viewing window along with half a dozen other people, mostly family members of the two victims he was convicted of murdering so heinously.

As she had watched he had turned his palé, thin face toward her and mouthed, *Why didn't you help me?*

Bastard. She hadn't helped him because he would not allow her to help. As soon as she had learned what really happened, she had attempted to have the verdict overturned—the verdict she had fought for and won.

Stop it. Enough. The whole thing was out of her hands. The execution had been stayed, which meant the governor of Texas would determine if the prisoner deserved a second chance to prove the innocence he initially denied. Whatever happened now was completely out of her hands.

She opened her eyes and refocused her attention on the man who claimed to be Paul Reyes. There was nothing about him that gave her reason to believe he was telling the truth. From his calloused palms to his manner of appearance, he did not fit the image her mind had shaped of an artist capable of creating such beauty on the canvas.

My line of work.

Then again, there were things about the man she had met last night that didn't quite fit, either. But she had chalked those up to differences in language, communication lapses. His few out-of-sync words were hardly reason to challenge his identity.

There was the way he had looked at her…as if she were the prey to be conquered and devoured. That had made her immensely uncomfortable. And that remark about fitness being important to his image.

That still nagged at her. Why would such an extreme recluse be concerned about his image? The idea shouldn't surprise her. Latin men were known for their machismo. But she'd discovered no indication that Paul Reyes operated with that attitude, but the files hadn't been all-inclusive.

Those few inconsistencies she had noticed last night did not mean that the man she'd met and with whom she'd talked shop had lied about who he was.

Since her captor still appeared to be sleeping, maybe she could try and use the telephone. There had to be one in here. What millionaire wanted to be stuck in his safe room with no way to call out?

"Have you made up your mind about me, Renee Parsons?"

His question made her jump. She hadn't realized he had opened his eyes and was staring at her. Perfect. There went her chances of looking for the telephone.

She dropped her feet to the floor and righted her twisted clothes. She cleared her throat and met that probing gaze. "I don't know how you think I could do that since you've given me no proof."

Another of those slow smiles she'd reluctantly admired tilted his lips. "Ah, yes, the proof."

He pushed to his feet and stretched. She followed his movements with far too much interest that could not be attributed to her assignment. Their commingled scents of warm flesh with a tang of fear thrown in had permeated the small space and had her feeling particularly out of sorts.

"I find this situation oddly amusing," he said with no hint of humor in his tone.

He reached for a pouch of water, offered one to her, but she shook her head. She was far more interested in what he had to say than she was in nourishing her body. She would probably regret it later.

He took a long drink, then explained, "Who would have considered that I might someday need to prove my own identity in such a way?" He gestured to the monitors. "This is my home and yet someone else has taken up residence here." He massaged his chin thoughtfully. "This is my face and yet another whose is so similar could claim what is mine as his own."

Renee sensed his desperation. His movements, his voice generated that sensation of near panic and yet he appeared calm to a degree that somehow lessened the hysteria quite clearly gnawing at him.

His gaze locked with hers. "You will believe what you choose. Your business with my brother, however, is another matter. I must know why you are here."

The tension filling the small room thickened, turned palpable. She could not deny how badly he wanted or needed to know what was going on, but from what perspective? Was Victor using her to bear witness to his theft of his brother's life? Is that why she was left here last night? If this man won her over, would she be confirming the wrong brother?

Was last night the same scenario from the other side of the coin? And yet, how could Victor or Paul Reyes have known who she was or when she would arrive? If she went with the theory that they could not have known, then all that had happened in conjunction with her arrival was coincidence.

She did not believe in coincidence.

Somehow, all or part of this chain of events had been meticulously planned. The only questions were by whom and how.

"My name is Renee Parsons," she stated for the record. "I represent a gallery in L.A. I came here to discuss art with Paul Reyes."

That dark gaze bored into hers and he moved, walked straight over to stand toe-to-toe with her. She trembled, but quickly grabbed back control.

"Then we have a problem, *Renee*," he said softly, the quiet words carrying a lethal message she couldn't miss. "Because I am certain my brother wants me dead. If, as you say, you are innocent in this grand scheme, I would surmise that as a witness to recent events, it is quite possible that he will want you dead, as well."

"Are you trying to frighten me, Mr. Reyes?" She inclined her head, searched those fathomless eyes. "It feels like that's exactly what you're doing."

"Yes," he confessed. "If that is what it takes to make you see the magnitude of this situation, then I will gladly terrify you."

Well, then, let the games begin. "I'm afraid we may have a problem," she said, not backing off even as he seemingly leaned nearer.

"And what is that, besides the obvious one, of course?"

His gaze flicked down to her lips. She shivered in spite of her determination not to.

"If you're Paul Reyes, as you say, then why should I be afraid? Paul Reyes is an artist who uses paint and a brush to pour out his emotions."

To her surprise, he reached behind him and produced a handgun, a .38 revolver. She hadn't seen that one coming. That put her right back at square one.

"Perhaps the artist has learned a hard lesson."

He stroked her cheek with the barrel of the weapon. Her lips compressed into a firm line, but she refused to allow the quake rumbling through her to surface.

"Why did you come here?" he demanded, the hand holding the weapon now hanging at his side. "Answer me truthfully and you will have nothing to fear."

If only it were that simple. She had no idea who this man was. He could be Victor attempting to determine her agenda. She could answer his question honestly and he could kill her here and now—if he was Victor.

"I came to do business with Paul Reyes."

Fury tightened his jaw. "Liar." He spat the word at her, those sculpted lips vibrating with the rage he felt.

"I tell you what," she countered, "why don't you paint me a picture and we'll settle this once and for all."

His nostrils flared with outrage. Oh, yes, that was what she needed. To see his real reactions. If this man was Victor Reyes, he would come unglued at her boldness. Victor had no use for women other than as sex objects. No way would he put up with her smart talk.

"You wish to inflame my fury. I understand your game, Ms. Parsons." He visibly calmed, or gave the impression of doing so. "But you have a valid point." He shoved the .38 into his waistband and grabbed her hand.

She didn't resist as he towed her toward the door. He surveyed the monitors for a moment, then entered a code and the door swung open.

Renee kept her victory cry to herself. She had accomplished her first goal: getting out of that tiny prison. If she were smart, the first chance she got she'd make a run for it. But then she still wouldn't know if he was Victor or Paul. She refused to fail in her first assignment. She had to stick with him for now. As soon as she found a way to contact Jim, she would give him an update on what she had learned so far. She needed to know why the DEA had shown up here. Had they been looking for Victor Reyes? What or who had tipped them off that he was here?

If he was here.

She arrowed a sideways glance at the man currently manacling her arm. Maybe they knew something she didn't.

Reyes led her through the bedroom and down the stairs. The entire house was a mess. Seeing the chaos firsthand made the reality all the more appalling.

Pausing at the front door, he glanced outside, then entered a sequence of digits into the security system keypad. The hurricane shutters on the windows slowly rolled upward, revealing the amazing views she had admired last evening.

The battered door and its damaged locks hung haphazardly from the hinges. He didn't bother trying to close it; it wouldn't have discouraged anyone who wanted to get inside. That was another thing. Why the hell hadn't the alarm gone off when the agents entered the house?

She stared back at the keypad even as Reyes lugged her along the entry hall.

"Why didn't the alarm go off when those men broke down the door?"

"The alarm for the exterior doors had been deactivated. That is why it did not go off when I entered the house."

That made sense, she supposed. But who deactivated it? She was pretty sure it was armed when she and Paul—the other Paul—attempted to escape.

By the time he stopped dragging her forward, they had moved through the great room and into what she would have called a sunroom overlooking the ocean, except that it was clearly a studio.

Paintings were propped against the wall all around the room. An easel with a fresh canvas sat in the middle of the space. Supplies lined shelves and probably filled the many drawers in the massive pieces of furniture positioned against one wall. As she passed the easel, she touched the blank canvas. Her fingertips came away dusty.

She swiped her palms together. "You planning a new painting?" Seemed as if he'd been in the planning stages quite a while, but then he'd said he'd been away.

"One day." He gestured to a small sofa. "Sit."

She wandered over to the sofa, curious to see what would happen next. The overstuffed yellow pillows welcomed her. Much better than the cot, she decided.

Reyes picked up a drawing pad and pencil and settled onto a stool a few feet away from her. He repositioned the .38 to the small of his back, the movement awkward somehow. He hung his feet on the rungs as if he'd sat this way a thousand times. The scruffy sneakers fit with the rest of his attire…but didn't work with the image of the man she'd formulated after studying his history. Could she have been that wrong about him? Or was her mind doing exactly what he wanted it to…buying into his story?

"Relax," he said, his gaze connecting with hers. "Most people like to play the part of subject."

She leaned back into the soft pillows and draped her arms along the back of the sofa in hopes of releasing the tension humming inside her. "I didn't know you worked with live subjects."

He lifted that dark gaze to hers. "Usually I don't." He let her think what she would and turned his attention back to his work.

His fingers were long and more slender than she'd noted before. She studied his movements for grace and dexterity. She saw both. Each time his gaze lifted to dissect some aspect of her face, her breath stilled. It was ridiculous, she knew, but somehow she couldn't help the reaction. Maybe it was being his subject. What girl hadn't fantasized once in her life about sitting for some great artist?

But this wasn't a fantasy. This was real. And the stakes were far too high for her to let him draw her into the engaging trap he was so carefully constructing.

"Do you always eat your lip that way?" Those eyes latched fully onto hers.

She stopped chewing her bottom lip as if she'd been caught hiding exculpatory evidence. "What?"

He licked his lips. "The way you bite your lip, do you always do that?" He stared at her mouth as he asked this.

"Is there a point to your question?" she demanded, flustered. What the hell did that have to do with anything? Why didn't he just draw the stupid picture so she could assess his talent?

He looked at her so long without speaking that she was sure he hadn't intended to. Then he said, "You don't realize your effect on men, do you?"

Okay, now he was really reaching. She got up. "This is crazy. Let me see what you've done."

"The drawing is not finished. Sit." He nodded to the sofa.

This wasn't going to prove anything if he kept toying with her. Was he buying time? What?

"I don't know what your goal is," she said, letting him hear the accusation in her tone, "but I know you're playing some kind of game and I don't like it. What's going on here?"

He slid off his stool, took the three steps necessary to stand directly in front of her. "Then we are at the same place, Renee Parsons, for I do not know what is going on here, either. Since this is my home—" he pounded his chest with his fist clutching the pencil "—my *life*, I would very much like to know the truth. Can you help me with that?"

For the first time since this insanity had started, she felt compelled to believe he might be telling her the truth.

She held out her hand. He stared at her palm and then, with only the briefest hesitation, he placed the drawing pad there. The image, as he'd said, was unfinished, but it was her. The likeness unmistakable, incredibly well done. If he wasn't Paul Reyes, he was damned good with a drawing pad and pencil.

"Do you believe me now?"

She held back the *yes*. "Maybe."

The muffled sound of doors slamming shattered the silence in the house.

"Someone is here," he whispered, echoing her thought.

He grabbed a remote from the table next to the sofa and turned on another of those plasma televisions camouflaged by a picture frame to look like wall art. The security screen came into focus. A black SUV was parked near her rental car and two men were getting out.

"Those look like the two guys from last night." She recognized the taller of the two without question...the second, she wasn't completely sure.

Reyes turned to her. "Go out this way." He gestured to the French doors that opened onto the rear patio. "Hide beneath the dock. You'll be safe there."

"What?" She dragged her attention from the screen. "What're you going to do?"

"Go," he urged as he withdrew the .38. "Go now!"

She didn't have time to formulate a reason not to do as he said, so she did exactly what he told her to do without looking back.

Chapter Six

Renee stopped at the bottom of the steps, flattened herself against the wall and slowed her breathing. She couldn't just run.

Had those men come back to kill her and Paul or Victor or whoever the hell he was?

She held her breath and listened.

The doors to the patio were open…maybe she could hear something. She'd give most anything for a weapon. They would take his .38…or maybe he would try to use it. Those guys would kill him. They were professionals. Burning fear seared through her.

"Put it down!"

Tension rippled through her. She remembered that voice from the night before. Definitely the same guy.

"Kick it across the floor."

Damn. There went the .38. At least he was cooperating. That would keep him alive for a while.

Would there be more weapons in the SUV belonging to these scumbags? A cell phone? OnStar?

Adrenaline firing through her veins, she moved to the corner of the house and surveyed the situation, then took off for the front of the house. The SUV was parked between her rental and the front steps. Maybe fifteen yards from her current position, with the tailgate facing her. There was nothing but open ground between her and the vehicle. It was a risk, but Reyes was probably dead if she didn't do something.

If he wasn't already. She hadn't heard any shots, but they could be using silencers.

She'd just summoned the courage to make the move to the SUV when a man exited the front of the house. Dressed in black just like last night, he rushed down the steps and to the vehicle.

She held her position, listened as much for his movements as anything coming from inside the house…like a scuffle or gunshot.

He opened the driver's side door and reached inside. When he drew back, he had retrieved a phone.

Well, there went her chance of borrowing his phone.

She tilted her head and strained to pay closer attention when he began to talk.

"Yes, we have him."

Pause.

"No. The woman is gone. He said she was gone when he arrived. Kicked her way out or something."

Her heart thumped. They hadn't just wanted her out of the way. There was more to it than that. How could that be? It felt as if they had been expecting her arrival. That wasn't possible...unless someone had double-crossed her. Double-crossed the Equalizers.

She needed to talk to Jim Colby.

"Yes. I'm certain."

Another pause, this one longer.

"Take him now?" Pause. "Yes, I understand."

He tossed the phone back into the vehicle and headed for the house.

Take him now?

Where would they be taking him? Back to Mexico?

She couldn't lose this guy. Whether he was Paul or Victor—and at the moment she was leaning toward the former—if she let him get away, she would fail and another innocent man would die.

She couldn't be responsible for that happening twice in one lifetime.

The idea that he'd lied to protect her by saying she was gone was another point on his side, but she didn't have time to worry about that right now.

Paul or Victor, she needed him. Preferably alive.

Without a second thought, she lunged for the rear of the SUV. She glanced toward the house. Still clear. Her hands shaking, she reached for the rear door. The SUV was an extended version with the side-by-side doors that opened into a large cargo space. The absence of a third-row seat made for more cargo room. There was a large bag, like a black plastic bag for yard trash, in one corner and a couple of shovels tossed in next to it.

She didn't have time to check out the contents or the bag or to dwell on the idea of why these creeps would be hauling around shovels. Careful of the shovels, she climbed inside and eased the door shut.

Did she have time to grab the phone? Check for a weapon?

Both?

Might as well take the time.

She started over the seat and voices coming from the front of the house had her ducking back down.

She curled up into the smallest ball possible, snuggled against the seat and then attempted to slide the bag in front of her. What the hell did they have in this bag? It weighed a ton.

The approach of footsteps had her pushing harder on the bag. It moved just enough to block most of her. It was at that exact instant that she considered that the two killers might just open the cargo doors and put Reyes back here. No way was she hidden well enough not to be seen if they opened those doors.

Why hadn't she thought of that?

She tugged at the bag, trying to pull herself more fully behind it. The plastic tore and she jerked her hand back, but it was too late; she'd made a gaping hole. She clamped her mouth shut and told herself not to even breathe.

From inside the bag, part of a face stared at her. An older man. Gray hair. Pale blue eyes. That was when she smelled it—death.

A scream burgeoned in her throat.

The rear passenger door opened. "Get in."

The growling voice was different from the guy's who'd made the phone call. The second man from last night.

She swallowed back the scream. Looked away from the bag as best she could without moving enough to make a sound.

The vehicle shifted as someone got into the backseat and the front seat simultaneously. Doors slammed. Seconds later, the front passenger door opened and someone else got in. The engine started as the final door closed.

Relief allowed the constriction around her chest to ease marginally. They weren't going to open the rear doors yet. Thank God.

"I can't exactly fasten my safety belt with my hands tied like this."

Renee's pulse hitched at the sound of Reyes's voice. If she reached up she could touch him, she realized. She dared to turn her face just enough to see the back of his head above the headrest.

"Maybe you'll get lucky," the killer who'd forced him into the backseat taunted, "and we'll crash before we get there. Save us the trouble of killing you."

Renee bit her lips together to stifle the gasp that caught in her throat.

They were going to kill him.

She had known that was a strong possibility, but to hear the words…

"Where are you taking me?"

"No questions." This from the driver, the man who'd made the phone call.

"Damn, do you smell that?" the man driving asked.

"We gotta bury that old bastard," the other one agreed.

No one said anything after that. Renee could hear the sounds of the city outside the vehicle each time he stopped for what she presumed was a traffic signal.

She wished she had the weapon they'd taken from her last night or the one Reyes had given up this morning. She wished there was a tire wrench in the cargo area instead of shovels and a dead body, but there wasn't.

No problem. She would just have to figure out another way to keep their plans from fruition.

If both killers got out at their destination, she could go for the phone in the front seat. But it would be too late for help to arrive and stop them from killing Reyes, not to mention her.

The self-defense classes she had taken after the kidnapping outside the courthouse, in her former career as a prosecutor, had helped her so far, but this was vastly different. There were two of these guys, and they both had guns. That one time she'd been held at gunpoint by the husband of a woman accused of overdosing her terminally ill father, she'd known that he wasn't really a killer. The man had simply been desperate to save his wife from a murder charge. All she'd had to do was stay calm and wait for an opportunity to disarm him.

This wasn't going to be nearly so simple.

Minutes crawled by. She watched out the rear window in hopes of getting some idea of where they were headed, but that didn't help. What she could see rarely changed, the sky interrupted only by power lines and the occasional building. The roar of the wheels on the pavement underscored the silence inside the vehicle.

She didn't know how much time passed, but the sky eventually gave way to trees. Lots of trees.

A forest.

Where would they go to find a forest this dense in south Florida?

Of course.

Everglades.

The realization dawned at the same time that Reyes finally spoke again.

"Why are we going into the park?"

Renee knew only two things about the Everglades: saw grass and alligators. Neither of which she wanted to know beyond pictures in a book.

When their abductors refused to answer, Reyes asked another question.

"What does my brother want?"

Why couldn't he say his brother's name? It would make her life so much simpler.

Yeah, right.

She was in the back of an SUV that was headed into the Everglades where a man would die and, evidently, where two would be buried. And the minute she was discovered, she would die, too.

Nothing about this was simple. Hadn't she been yearning for complex?

Be careful what you wish for….

"He wants you dead," the front passenger said with a chuckle. "Then, when they find what's left of your body, there won't be enough to cause any trouble."

Oh, hell.

Renee swallowed the bitter taste of bile.

Her first assignment, and she was going to get herself killed. Jim Colby had been right; maybe she hadn't been up for this one.

No. She refused to give up.

Stay calm. Pay attention. There's always hope.

All she had to do was look for the opportunity.

"He doesn't possess the courage to take care of this personally?"

Renee winced. Was Reyes trying to get these guys ticked off? Not that anything he said or did at this point was going to stop the inevitable, but there was no need to hurry it along.

"He doesn't like wasting his time."

"Or getting his hands dirty," Reyes suggested in a bitter, scathing tone that said more about how he felt about his brother than any words could.

He really was bucking for a battle. The man was unarmed and tied up. These two jerks were going to kill him because his brother had ordered the hit. Now was not the time to be mouthing off.

"Shut up," the driver ordered.

Reyes said nothing more.

Renee allowed some of the tension to seep out of her muscles. She would need all her energy to figure a way out of this.

The vehicle slowed and took a turn. The road felt rougher now. A side road deeper into the park? She didn't know. She'd never been here before. Didn't want to be here now.

The trees were so thick at this point that it was like dusk outside, and it wasn't even ten o'clock in the morning yet. She worked at keeping her breathing slow and soundless. With the conversation at a standstill inside the vehicle she couldn't afford to have anyone hear her breathing erratically. Besides, she had no desire to inhale any more of the poor dead man's stench than necessary for survival.

She thought of how she had been betrayed and how devastated she had been. She'd worked that case alongside her mentor, Austin's esteemed district attorney who had visions of becoming a Texas senator. She'd admired and respected him. Her primary goal had been to achieve the kind of legendary status he had in his distinguished career. But she'd made a mistake. He hadn't been the great man she'd thought he was. In the end, no one had believed her. He had lied and an innocent man had been ushered into Texas's infamous fast lane to execution.

But her revered mentor wasn't the only one who had betrayed her. *He* had as well. He had allowed her to hate him…to believe the worst about him. To protect her.

And now her brother was on death row, alive this day only by virtue of the last-minute decision of the governor of Texas.

She blinked back the sting of tears. Sometimes she hated him for what he'd done. Other times, she wanted to break into that damned prison and rescue him the way she'd rescued him a million times as a scrawny kid.

I've never done one damned thing right in my entire life. Just let me do this one thing right, Sis. That's all I ask.

The idiot! How could he have believed that confessing to murders he hadn't committed was doing the right thing? For God's sake! And not just any murder. Two of the most heinous killings in Austin history. The whole state had wanted someone to blame.

Stupid, stupid.

How could her own brother have been that stupid?

They hadn't spoken for months after he'd been arrested. She had hated his drug use and inability to pull his life together for so long that she didn't remember the last time she'd thought of him in a favorable light.

Though she hadn't been primary on the case, she'd supported her boss. The press had eaten up the idea that the suspected murderer's own sister had helped present the case against him.

Damn him for letting her do that. Damn her for not letting it go…she just had to keep digging until she found the truth. And then he silenced her. She'd had no choice but to walk away.

The SUV came to a stop and Renee's attention snapped back to the present. Judging by the even thicker canopy of trees, they were deep in the middle of nowhere.

The front doors opened and the vehicle shifted as the two scumbags in charge of this outing got out. She held her breath, hoped they wouldn't open the rear door just yet. She needed an opportunity first. Just in case, her fingers curled around the handle of the closest shovel. She might die in the next few minutes but, by God, she would go down fighting like a wildcat.

The rear passenger door opened. "Get out."

Reyes followed the order without comment.

The door slammed shut.

Renee lay very still for a moment. Then another.

They were going to kill him. Then they'd come for the dead guy and the shovels.

She had to do something.

Fear pounding in her chest, she raised herself up into a partial sitting position and peered over the seat. Outside, a few yards from the front of the vehicle, the two men stood, their backs to her. Reyes waited beyond their position, facing the two bastards with the guns, his hands tied behind him.

There was only one thing she could do.

Now or never.

She climbed over the rear seat, her gaze not leaving the men. Slowly, afraid she'd make a sound, she levered herself over the console and into the driver's seat. She scooted down low so that her head wouldn't be a target. Her fingers were icy as they closed around the key in the ignition.

Do it, she ordered, or he dies.

She twisted the key. The engine started.

One of the killers shouted something like, "What the hell?"

She rammed the gearshift into Drive and stomped the accelerator.

The SUV lunged forward.

More shouting.

She hoped like hell Reyes had the good sense to get out of the way.

She peeked above the dash just in time to see that she'd run out of road and was about to barrel into the woods.

She cut the wheel right and braked hard.

The vehicle careened sideways, cutting through underbrush.

A teeth-jarring stop later, she scrambled out the door, hesitated long enough to grab the cell phone that had flown into the floorboard and ran like hell. The dense forest swallowed her up.

The shouting behind her was too close for comfort.

She had to run faster.

Underbrush slapped at her legs. She ignored it. Faster. Harder. She couldn't stop.

Gunshots exploded in the air.

She weaved right and then left.

She couldn't tell if they were shooting at her or at Reyes.

No time to look back.

Run.

Her heart slammed mercilessly against her ribcage.

Don't look back.

Don't stop.

Or you'll die.

Chapter Seven

Jim Colby checked the time again. More than thirty hours since he'd heard from Vaughn. He was worried. She should have connected with Paul Reyes by now. And she should have checked in again.

He'd contacted DEA Agent Joseph Gates at 5:00 a.m. this morning. Gates was supposed to check out the situation and get back to him, but that was hours ago. If he didn't hear from Vaughn or Gates by midnight, he was going down there.

Maybe the thing going on with her brother had her too distracted. He'd hoped putting her on a case would help. That might have been a mistake. She hadn't told him about the situation with her brother; he'd found that out on his own. He'd known something was going on with her. He'd made a few calls, reached out to some of his contacts at the FBI and with the U.S. Marshals. It might not help, but it couldn't hurt. He knew people in high places through his mother, and her agency was a useful tool. According to his sources, Vaughn's brother, Matthew, had confessed to the murders but Vaughn had insisted he was innocent—even after initially helping present the case against him. But something or someone had shut her up, ultimately causing her to leave Texas. If there was a way to help Vaughn's brother, the people he knew could make it happen.

The telephone rang and Jim grabbed the receiver. Connie and the others had gone home a couple of hours ago.

"Colby."

"The situation down here doesn't look good."

Joseph Gates.

Jim tensed. "What do you have?"

"We've had an internal snafu."

Jim scrubbed at his forehead. This was not the news he'd wanted to hear. "What the hell kind of snafu?"

"According to the briefing I just sat through," Gates began, "a fellow agent's contact in Marathon called in the impending arrival of a private aircraft from a small airfield on Mexico's Yucatán Peninsula shortly after midnight this a.m. The aircraft refueled and returned immediately to Mexico, but this gung-ho agent got there in time to snap some covert photos. The single passenger was listed as a George

Gonzales. But imagery analysis confirmed that it was Victor Reyes."

Tension roiled in Jim's gut. "And?" There was more. All of it bad, if the vibes he was picking up from Gates were any indication.

"Rather than going through the regular channels, my knuckleheaded colleague assembled an assault team and moved in on the residence of Paul Reyes in Key Largo. Victor Reyes was suspected of having gone straight there from the airfield."

Jim swore repeatedly under his breath.

"My sentiments exactly," Gates muttered.

"Where's Vaughn?" Jim braced for the worst. He should never have assigned her to this case. But the idea of bringing down a major drug lord was high on her priority list of things to do in her new career. Whether she admitted it or not, it was likely due to her brother's troubles with drugs. Initially Jim hadn't seen any problem with giving her the case. She was female, a necessary requirement to get the job done. She was prepared. All she had to do was get close to Paul Reyes. When the time was right, he and Johnson, along with Agent Gates, would have assisted in the takedown of Victor Reyes. It wasn't supposed to happen like this.

"Don't know. The house was empty. No sign of foul play other than a hole in the wall in a room in the basement. Vaughn's purse was found in the residence, and her rental car is still parked outside. No blood. No bodies. No nothing."

Fury knotted inside Jim. "How the hell did this happen, Gates? I thought you said this case was off the books. That you were doing this dark."

"We're grilling the agent involved just to make sure he wasn't somehow connected to Victor. Hell, Jim, I don't know the answer. I'll do everything I can on this end to find Vaughn."

That just wasn't good enough. Jim clenched his teeth to hold back the words.

"The good news is," Gates offered, "Victor Reyes is here somewhere. All we have to do is find the SOB."

"Yeah." A determined fury ignited deep in Jim's gut. "Keep me posted." Gates agreed to keep him informed and Jim hung up the phone. For several seconds, he stared at it.

Whatever had gone down with the DEA, it wasn't on the up-and-up. If Jim discovered that Gates was playing him, there wouldn't be any place on this damned planet the bastard could hide. But that would have to wait. For now, he needed to do what he could for Vaughn. He needed eyes and ears where this was going down. He needed someone on her side. Gates was supposed to have been his immediate backup on this in case anything went wrong. He'd failed. He was no longer dependable.

Jim picked up the phone once more and entered the contact number for his newest associate, Sam Johnson. Johnson picked up after the third ring.

"This is Jim Colby." He paused a moment to give Johnson a chance to turn down the volume of the music playing in the background. "We have a situation," Jim explained. "I'd like you to do what you do best."

A few minutes later, after laying out the situation, Jim placed the receiver back into its cradle. Sam Johnson was a former forensics expert. If there was anything to be found where Vaughn had been since her arrival in Florida, he would find it. Having him on site would also allow for immediate action in the event Vaughn needed him.

Damn it. This wasn't supposed to happen. Vaughn was only supposed to get to know Paul Reyes. Once she got close enough, he would have been used to lure Victor to this country. After all, Paul was Victor's only living family. According to Gates, Victor was protective of his brother despite present circumstances. The plan had been well thought out; nothing was supposed to have gone wrong.

How the hell had this gone to hell so fast and furiously?

A buzz signaled that someone was at the front entrance of the brownstone that served as the offices for the Equalizers. Surprised at having anyone show up this late, Jim stood. Wouldn't be Tasha, she had a key. Could be a customer, he supposed, even at this hour. He didn't bother turning off the light as he left his office. If it was a customer he'd be right back.

At the bottom of the stairs, he flipped the switch that lit the wall sconces in the lobby. He crossed to the door, unlocked and opened it.

"Did I catch you on your way out?" Victoria Colby-Camp asked with a skeptical look on her face.

Forcing his tension to recede, he mustered an amiable tone. "I was just about to call it a night." He stepped back, opened the door wider. His mother had not come all the way across town at a time when she was usually relaxing with an after-dinner glass of wine with her husband unless she wanted to talk. "Come on in. We can talk while I square away my office."

Victoria stepped into the lobby and he closed up behind her. Since she knew the way to his office as well as he did, she preceded him up the stairs. The distinguished navy suit with matching pumps was classic Victoria. As usual, not a hair was out of place. His mother, whether commanding the troops at her private investigations agency or seeing after his six-month-old daughter, was always poised and in charge. Just one of the things he loved about her.

In his office, she made herself comfortable while he cleared his desk. She would get around to whatever she had on her mind in her own time. He'd learned patience since crashing back into his mother's life.

"Tasha tells me you haven't been home for dinner a single night this week."

So that was what this impromptu visit was about. "I have a couple of sensitive cases going right now." He met her scrutinizing gaze. "I'm sure you understand." Jim didn't remember much about his early childhood; most of his memories before age eight had been so thoroughly wiped or corrupted that, were it not for a couple of good psychiatrists, he might not have any. Months of intensive therapy, and a few special treatment sessions he'd just as soon not repeat, had extracted enough recall for him to know that his parents had loved him dearly. He had lost that knowledge for a lot of years. Hatred and bitterness had consumed him during that time.

But that was behind him now.

"Jim," his mother said, her eyes worried, her tone weary, "I know this new venture is extremely important to you. No one wants the Equalizers to succeed more than me." She sighed. "But I see you making the same mistake your father and I made twenty-odd years ago."

This surprised him. "Mistake?" He understood that his mother still blamed herself for his kidnapping, but that was unfair to her. She'd had no idea what the man who had stolen him away from his home was capable of. How could she? What had happened was not her fault, nor was it his father's. It had taken two decades for him to understand that, but he knew it now.

She held his gaze with desperation in her own

when he would have shifted his attention back to the papers on his desk. "Your father and I were so fixated on getting the Colby Agency off the ground back then that we didn't pay attention as closely as we should have to what mattered most. We likely missed warning signs that evil was about to strike. It was a mistake."

"Mom." Jim rested his hands on his desk, leaned in her direction and poured all the assurance he possessed into what he was about to say. "You didn't do anything wrong. Leberman–" he hated saying the name out loud, he despised even thinking it "—wasn't going to stop until he'd hurt you and Dad." He didn't use the more familiar terms very often, but she needed to hear them just now.

Her deep shuddering breath told him exactly how much the past still weighed upon her. Then she stood, straightened her suit jacket and smiled as if she'd put it behind her and moved on all in one breath.

"You're right, son, I know that." She glanced pointedly at the clock before meeting his gaze again. "Just don't take your family for granted. You might turn around at the least expected moment and find someone you love gone. You'll ask yourself what was the last thing you said or did, and it won't be right or enough. And you won't ever be able to make it right or enough."

"I hear what you're saying." She'd given him this speech a couple of dozen times recently. "How's the construction going?" Might as well shift the subject to her and her "baby."

She smiled. "The Colby Agency is rising from the ashes right on schedule. We should be moving in by September."

That was one of the things he loved most about his mother—she was unstoppable. No matter how hard life got, she just kept on charging ahead.

"Outstanding."

She skirted his desk and kissed him on the cheek. "Now, go home. Your wife and daughter need to spend time with you."

His mother was right. "Give me a minute. I'll walk out with you."

He was going home. Johnson would find Vaughn…if she wasn't dead already.

If she was, some-damned-one would pay.

Chapter Eight

It was so damned dark.

Renee was positive that she was in the clear at this point.

Problem was, she didn't have a clue where she was.

She'd been running for hours.

Peering down at the cell phone's screen, she resisted the impulse to shout *yes*. Finally she had service. Only two bars, but it could work.

After entering the number for the office, she held her breath as she waited for the call to go through.

"Colby."

Relief made her knees weak.

"Jim, it's Renee."

"Vaughn?"

His voice was broken.

Damn it. Not a good connection.

She looked at the screen, moved first one way and then the other until the second bar appeared once more. Then she froze.

"Can you hear me okay now?"

"There's some static, but go ahead. Are you safe?"

Renee resisted the urge to look around the dark woods. "I'm in the Everglades. Two of Victor's men tried to kill us and we're on foot. Otherwise, I'm good to go." She was fairly certain that the man who'd been with her was Paul. As sure as she could be, anyway.

"Is Paul Reyes with you?"

"He's out here somewhere, just not with me."

"Are Victor's men still on your trail?"

"Possibly."

"Is this your cell phone?"

"No, I lifted it from one of the guys who brought us here."

"Okay, listen to me carefully, Vaughn."

She took a deep breath, let it out slowly.

"The men who are after you may use this phone to track you. So as soon as we're finished here I want you to turn the phone off and don't turn it on again unless it's an emergency."

"Got it."

"Now, give me as many details as you can about your location."

"Paul mentioned a park. He said something like,

'why are we going into the park?' We weren't on the road that long after leaving Key Largo. Maybe thirty or forty minutes."

"Anything else?"

She racked her brain. "No. Nothing I can recall."

"All right. I assume you don't have supplies."

"Just the phone."

Saying it out loud made the idea sound even worse.

"There are park rangers throughout the area. Find a ranger's station if you can and you'll find supplies. I don't want to send a search party in there for you unless it's absolutely necessary. Johnson's on the ground down there. I'll see what he can do. Maybe he and a guide can find you and bring you out."

He didn't have to explain his reasons for not wanting to send a search party. That would require bringing Gates up to speed.

"It's someone in the DEA, isn't it? That's where this thing went wrong," she asked. Her mission should have been simple. She should be wining and dining Paul Reyes right now, not running for her life in a swamp.

A moment of silence lapsed. "Why do you say that?" her boss inquired noncommittally.

"Those guys were all over the Key Largo residence just minutes after Paul arrived from Mexico. They had to have been given advance notice. Something was wrong with the whole situation."

"You've lost me, Vaughn. What do you mean after Paul arrived from Mexico?"

She filled him in on the events of the past twenty-four hours and wrapped up with, "I think Victor is trying to pin his whole sick existence on his brother so he can walk away with a clean slate and a new life."

"Find Paul Reyes if he's still alive," Jim ordered, "and lie low as long as you can. Keep him in the dark, if possible. He might not cooperate if he learns why you're down there."

She'd decided to go that route already.

"Look," she began, hoping like hell she had the guts to see this through, "if we make it out of here alive, I don't want to get ambushed by the DEA. This may sound crazy, but maybe you should keep Johnson on top of Gates. He's the only one who knew I was coming. This all happened almost immediately after I arrived at Paul's residence. The whole setup seemed to have been arranged for me to believe that Paul had been kidnapped by his brother's henchman. But there was a glitch. Somehow Paul showed up and screwed up the plan."

"All right. But if you get into trouble, use this phone. I don't want you dead, Vaughn. Do you hear me?"

"Yeah, I hear you." She looked around again, trying her best to peer through the blanket of night. "If I can find Paul, and he's still alive, we'll get out of here somehow."

She ended the call and shut down the phone

before sliding it into her bra strap. The slacks she wore had no pockets, so her choices were limited.

Drawing in a deep breath, she scanned the darkness around her. Despite her brave talk to Jim, if she got out of this alive it would be a miracle.

It would be nice if the moonlight could cut more effectively through the canopy of trees, but that was wishful thinking in this jungle. The mosquitoes hummed around her as if she were the dinner buffet on tonight's menu. She slapped at her neck. What she would give for some insect repellent.

She had been moving in a sweeping pattern in hopes of encountering Paul. So far she hadn't encountered anything that wasn't indigenous to the area. Resting for a bit, while she was still on dry land, would most likely be the smart thing to do. He could be close by. Maybe he would catch up if she took a breather.

Not knowing where the forest merged with the ocean of muck and saw grass was her biggest concern. She had no desire to find that territory. Her sense of direction had worked fairly well so far. If her luck held out, she might just make it until daylight without running upon anything that hadn't had dinner tonight.

Dread settled heavily in the pit of her stomach when she considered that Reyes might very well be dead. Those scumbags had fired off several rounds. That could mean they hadn't hit their target. Or maybe it meant they hadn't got her in addition to their primary target. She'd have to operate under the assumption that Paul was out here somewhere, maybe even looking for her.

Giving up was something she had no intention of doing…again.

As her breathing slowed since she was no longer moving in a dead run, she grew more aware of the night sounds around her. Frogs calling in loud, deep voices, and the high-pitched cry of insects. Once in a while the hoot of an owl or the splashing of water would jerk her attention one way or the other.

She tried to shake the shivers, but that wasn't happening this side of sunrise. As long as she was out here in the dark, her imagination was going to work overtime. Though she had never visited the Everglades, she had some idea of the range of animal species that called this habitat home. The only friendly ones, as far as she was concerned, were the white-tailed deer and the various types of birds.

Snakes, spiders, alligators, to name a few, were not exactly her choices in roommates.

But there was no avoiding the residents here. She'd done her share of camping as a kid, so she wasn't entirely out of her element in this setting. Just out of her comfort zone.

Rest a few minutes and start out again fresh. Find Reyes and select a place to lie low until the dust settled. Victor Reyes was somewhere in Florida, and someone in the DEA appeared to be on his side. Maybe she was jumping the gun, but she'd learned her lesson about trusting the so-called good guys. She was sticking with the facts. Namely, Gates was the only person in Florida who had known her mission details, when and where, et cetera. All hell had broken loose, and here she was trekking her way through the wilderness with killers on her tail.

Since there were no other facts to refute those two, she had to go with that scenario. Someone in the DEA, either Gates or someone he'd entrusted with this information, was dirty.

She used her foot to tamp the ground around her chosen tree that would serve as a temporary lounge. Then, her heart thundering foolishly, she crouched down and felt around with her hand. Damp and cool earth interrupted only by the exposed, tangled roots of a tree she couldn't identify in the dark, but no critters that she could readily recognize by touch.

Carefully, she eased down into a sitting position and leaned against the gnarled tree. A scurry through the underbrush to her right snapped her attention in that direction. Snake? Too noisy. Gator? Too light. Bird? Maybe. Which ones were nocturnal? She couldn't recall. Well, except for the owls.

She sat perfectly still and listened, allowing her muscles to relax after hours of brutal punishment running through the wilds with nothing but dainty sandals for protecting her feet.

The whisper of something solid slipping through vegetation was unmistakable. What sounded like a muffled footstep, then another.

Goose bumps rose on her skin.

This could be company.

Human company.

Something upright for sure.

Were there bears in the Everglades?

Maybe.

She eased into a crouch and braced for defending herself. Part of her wanted to run like hell. Stay very, very still, her more rational brain cells ordered.

Keeping still won out.

She didn't even breathe.

Closer. The interloper moved slowly but steadily. Just one, she decided.

Almost upon her now.

She prepared to launch an attack.

Her heart practically stopped when whatever it was rushed through the underbrush behind her and just kept going.

A deer. She hadn't been able to see it, of course. It was dark, and the animal had been behind her. But she was sure it was a deer.

Or a panther.

A chill went through her.

There weren't that many panthers around anymore, but there were still a few.

Whatever kind of creature, it was gone now.

She relaxed.

Five more minutes and then she would restart her search for Paul.

Her eyes started to grow heavy. She jerked them open and got to her feet. If she kept sitting there, she would fall asleep. Might as well start moving again.

A hand abruptly clamped over her mouth.

Renee screamed, but the sound was trapped in her throat.

She scrambled to get away, but a strong arm hauled her up against a solid body.

"Do not be afraid, Renee."

She stilled.

Reyes. Paul.

As she pushed his hands away, she turned to face him, for all the good it would do in the dark. "What the hell do you mean sneaking up on me like that?"

"Keep your voice down," he whispered.

She shut up. Listened. Even the frogs and insects had gone silent in expectation of trouble.

"I thought you were dead," she snapped, suddenly and irrationally frustrated that he wasn't, or maybe because he'd caught her off guard.

"I thought I was, too."

Okay, calm down.

"Are they still out there looking for us?" she whispered. The idea that they might give up for the night was probably just a pipe dream.

"I don't think so." His body was very close to hers.

Close enough for her to feel the heat from his skin. "But we should proceed as if they are out there."

He was right. She wouldn't have made any noise at all if he hadn't scared the hell out of her.

"How did you find me?" she demanded. It was dark. They were in a swamp. His vision and hearing couldn't be *that* good.

"I have followed you for hours. I did not want to get too close until I was sure it was safe to do so."

She supposed that made sense. He'd had the advantage, after all, since he'd been behind her.

"Were those Victor's men in the SUV?" They were the same guys who'd manhandled her the night before. The same ones who'd taken the first man who'd claimed to be Paul Reyes. The more she thought about that whole strange event, the more she was certain she had been set up. It all had happened far too conveniently.

"My brother's men. Felipe and Rafael. His personal bodyguards."

She supposed it shouldn't surprise her that he knew them by name. "They were going to kill you."

"Yes. They killed my caretaker, as well. I had feared as much when I returned to find my home in…such condition."

The man in the garbage bag. She shivered. Poor guy.

"So, he really is trying to assume your identity?" she asked as if she still couldn't believe it. That was her conclusion, based on the few available facts, but for now he didn't need to know what she knew.

"Yes, it would seem so."

The resignation in his voice made her feel sad for him. She knew exactly how it felt to have your brother use you. His scumbag brother provided the drugs, and her stupid brother used them. Both uncaring about the lives they ruined. The whole idea stank.

The silence went on a little too long. If she were going to keep her cover in place, there were questions he would probably expect her to ask.

"We should probably hole up here for the night unless we have company." If they kept moving, they could run into real trouble that had nothing to do with Victor's men.

"I agree. Continuing to move around in the dark will only get us more lost."

With that decision out of the way, it was time for those expected questions.

"Why does your brother want to kill you and assume your identity?"

"To escape his past." He tugged her downward as he settled onto the ground.

She didn't mind sharing a tree with him, but it did make for close quarters. "You've been estranged for years?" she asked, pushing on with her questioning.

"Yes. He resided in Mexico. I lived here." He

exhaled a heavy breath. "Until I could no longer ignore the needs of my people."

She remembered he had said that.

"About one year ago, I began spending more and more time in Mexico."

That, she had to admit, made sense. A few of the more recent paintings she'd seen were of historic churches and quaint villages, when most of his other work centered on the water and the sky. One particular scene of the sunset on the water was her favorite. The color and detail were so vivid. Breathtaking. She thought of his calloused hands, and she felt an ache deep inside for the man who would risk those talented hands to help others. Startled, she dismissed the sensation.

"You hired this caretaker to see after your home in Key Largo while you were away?"

"Mr. Harbin. I called him frequently enough to ensure all was as it should be. The past six months in particular, I was unable to get home, but all appeared to be well. Until one month ago. I was unable to reach Harbin."

When his brother had imprisoned him in their childhood home in Merida.

"In all your trips to Mexico, you never ran into Victor?"

"No. My brother maintains a home somewhere in Mexico City. Even I do not know where. He prefers his anonymity."

That answer certainly went along with what she knew about Victor Reyes.

Silence elapsed between them, but the world beyond their tree trunk was anything but silent. The insects seemed to cry out for something only they understood; the nearly constant high tempo was punctuated by the rhythmic bass of the frogs.

"Tell me about your childhood." She didn't really need to know about his early life, but it seemed to be a reasonable question, one she would ask a new acquaintance under other circumstances. "Was your family wealthy?" That they owned property and a staff was maintained spoke of money.

"My family was wealthy enough. We had what we required and more."

"Your parents are still alive?"

She knew the answer to that one, but she would be asking it as well as a number of others. He couldn't know that she knew. Their roles had reversed. He had held her hostage on some level at his home for a few short hours, but now he was her hostage, in a manner of speaking. She would be in charge of their movements, as much to protect him as to use him. If Victor Reyes opted to stay hidden, whether on American soil or not, they would need Paul to lure him out of hiding.

Her mission was back to where it should be. Keeping Paul Reyes close at hand. Encouraging him to trust her. Until they had his brother in custody.

"No, they died. There is only Victor and me. We were happy as children. There were the usual sibling rivalries. Nothing…dramatic."

His hesitation made her wonder what he'd just remembered. "Why does he want to steal your life?"

A beat of silence. "Because he is afraid."

"What causes his fear?" she pushed.

More of that deep silence.

"Sorry," she offered. "I shouldn't have asked."

"He barters in illegal goods."

That was putting it kindly, in her opinion.

"What does that mean, exactly?" Too much prying would definitely give her away, but this seemed like a logical question. So far, she appeared to have gained some ground in the area of trust.

"Drugs."

"As in cocaine or something like that?" she ventured.

"Yes."

"I'm sure your parents were devastated with his decision to become a part of that world."

"They died many years before that," he corrected. "They were killed in a boating accident. We were on vacation. My brother and I were the only survivors."

That had to have been horrifying. "How old were you?"

"Twelve. My brother was fourteen."

Renee couldn't imagine being left all alone at

that age. "Who took care of you? Did you have other family?"

"No other family. We were raised by the caretakers of our family home."

She wondered if the reason Paul painted all those waterscapes was because his parents had died in the water. Asking would be too personal.

"Why were you in the SUV?" He opened up his own line of questioning. "I told you to hide."

Tension vibrated along her nerve endings. What she heard in his voice sounded a little like suspicion. She couldn't fault him there. In his shoes, she would be pretty damned suspicious.

"What do you mean?"

"Why would you take such a risk to save a man who had held you at gunpoint just a few hours ago? That seems out of character for an art buyer."

She winced. She would need a damned good answer for that one.

"I couldn't do it," she admitted. "I got around the house and intended to make a run for the gate," she fabricated, "when I heard one of the men make a call. He said something about taking you somewhere. I was afraid they were going to hurt you, so I did the only thing I could think of. I hid in the vehicle."

She took a breath, hoped her explanation would allay his suspicions.

The sounds of nature filled the lull that dragged on for a couple of minutes.

He was thinking, she decided. Trying to determine if her responses were reasonable. She could see how her actions looked a little suspicious. She'd gone after defendants for less.

"So you set out to rescue me, did you?"

The amusement had trumped the suspicion. Good. "Yes. I suppose I did, though I had no idea how I would manage it or exactly why I would need to." She relaxed a fraction. She'd barely skated out of that one.

"The expression on the faces of those men was quite priceless when the SUV's engine suddenly started."

She bit her lower lip a second. "I didn't consider that I might run over you in the process. I just knew I had to do something fast."

"Understandable. I headed for the trees the moment their attention shifted to the vehicle. Your timing was remarkable."

"Luck," she admitted. "I was desperate. At that point, I knew they were going to kill you." He didn't need to know that she'd utilized the only weapon at her disposal. Luck had nothing to do with it. It was about thinking on her feet.

"I take it you believe I am who I say I am at this point."

He was looking at her, or at least his face was turned toward her. She looked at him, in his direction, anyway. She could vaguely make out his form, but she couldn't really see him. Nor could he see her, she would wager. That he wanted to sense her total reaction should have concerned her, but it didn't. She was confident of her standing with him now.

"I'm convinced you're telling me the truth."

"Was it the drawing?"

"That was part of it."

"Ah, but I could still be lying," he countered. "Perhaps Victor has a gift for drawing. Drawing and painting are very different."

The hair on the back of her neck lifted, not from fear but from anticipation. He was enjoying this sparring with her. "You could be, yes."

"But you do not believe I am."

"No, I don't believe you are."

"As you said before, you have no real proof."

"True," she confessed. "But I can't imagine why an artist who creates such beauty would want to kill his own brother or anyone else. And you're definitely the artist in the family."

More of that silence that was filled with a thousand sounds.

"It's more than the drawing," she went on when it likely wasn't necessary. "It was the way you held the pencil…the way your fingers moved with each stroke of the lead against the paper."

Maybe she'd said a little more than was necessary. She shifted her attention forward, drew her knees up to her chest and wrapped her arms around them. "Anyway, I believe you're Paul Reyes."

"You saved my life, I am in your debt."

He was closer somehow…leaning toward her. If she turned toward him now…no, she couldn't do that. Too close—way too close. But the desire to do so was strong. She shivered.

"Are you cold?"

"No."

"When this is done, perhaps I may be able to properly show my gratitude."

That was an invitation for more than simply dinner. Didn't take a crystal ball to pick up on that. She would have had to be deaf not to have noted the nuances of hope and desire and plain old lust in his deep voice.

"You do understand that I'm asking you to my home for a social occasion," he clarified. "That is not something I do often."

"Yes…I understand. I'm just…considering what to say."

He laughed softly. "I am afraid that if you feel compelled to consider what to say, then the answer is perhaps not one I wish to hear."

She laughed, couldn't help the response. Maybe because she was tired…maybe because he was so close, she couldn't get a grip on her emotions. "The answer is yes, okay?"

"Yes. Okay. That is a good answer."

Nature's music crowded in around them again. For the first time since he'd grabbed her in the dark, she felt totally exhausted. She needed sleep, but the threat that could still be out there made her second-guess the idea. Victor's men could show up any second.

"Are you worried that Victor's men will find us?"

He picked up on her feelings far too easily. "The thought crossed my mind."

"We could take turns sleeping."

"That could work."

"You sleep first, I'll keep watch."

Tempting, but letting down her guard wouldn't be a good move. "I'm not sure—"

"Wait. You will sleep better if you are comfortable." He wrapped those long fingers around the arm closest to him and before she could fathom his intent he'd ushered her into his lap. "You saved my life. This is the least I can do for you."

Incredibly, she got the distinct impression that he meant exactly what he said. Had any other guy made this move, she would have been certain he was only trying to get her in his lap.

"Really, I'm okay."

She started to scoot away, but he closed his arms around her and drew her to his solid chest. "This is good. Sleep. Morning will be here before you know it. We will have quite a walk ahead of us."

Or run, she added silently, if Victor's men found their trail again.

Her cheek rested against his shoulder, her face

turned into his neck. She would be lying if she said this wasn't much better. This was…great.

"I fear they will look for us again when it is daylight," he added softly. He sounded resigned to the possibility.

"I think you're right. We have to be prepared for that possibility."

He'd lived here for years. Had recognized that those men were bringing him to the park. Maybe he knew the area.

"Can you find your way out of here?" she asked, hopeful.

"Perhaps."

She bit her lip and sighed wearily. If he thought he knew the way out of here, he would want to lead. She'd have to find a way to deal with that in the morning.

He laughed softly, the sound rumbled deep in his chest. "We will find our way out, or the park rangers will find us. I suspect that is why my brother's men gave up so quickly. The sound of gunfire carries. The fear of being caught by park authorities may have hastened their concession to defeat, at least for the moment."

He'd taken her sigh as worry. Good. "You're right, they're probably long gone for the night."

"You may sleep then, no?"

Sleep. In his lap with his arms around her? Definitely no. She lied, "Yes, thank you." Her body was beginning to heat up in places that weren't conducive to sleep. He appeared to have the same problem, judging by some of the contours nudging her backside. But he was right—if she didn't rest she would be no good tomorrow. Just as he wouldn't be.

Sleep, she ordered. Don't think about his body and the way it felt to be this close to him.

If only those frogs and crickets or whatever they were would lull her to sleep. Things would be much clearer in the morning.

As long as she didn't wake up dead.

Chapter Nine

Friday, May 4th, time unknown

He woke with a start.

Dawn had crept its way through the trees and offered enough light for him to barely make out his surroundings. He had not intended to fall asleep, but exhaustion had eventually claimed him. If Victor's men had not found them by then, he doubted they were still looking in the dark. However, with dawn's arrival, the search would begin anew. Nothing would be left to chance.

He could not be certain, but he sensed that he and Renee were still amid the thirty-eight acres considered traversable park land. This could be helpful. Park rangers frequently roved the area. The chances for rescue were quite significant, whether he could find the way out or not.

This was good.

The woman in his arms still slept soundly. She

would need her strength and her courage to make the journey back to a more civilized trail. There were many trails and narrow roads; it was only a matter of finding one before his brother's men found them.

Perhaps he underestimated her. She had, after all, climbed into that SUV with the intention of doing what she could to help him.

She snuggled against him, the movement of her soft body arousing his to the point of pain. He held his breath until the near overwhelming sensations eased.

On one level, he did not fully trust her, but on all others he wanted to learn all there was to know about her. Her heroic efforts to go out of her way to help him were troubling, as was the timing of her arrival. He could not disprove that she was an art buyer from Los Angeles as she claimed, but her arrival at his home at the same time his brother decided to put his scheme into action seemed too large a coincidence. That she had not run while she had the chance on not one but two occasions did not bode well for her complete innocence in this puzzling scenario. Surely a mere art buyer would have fled for her life at the first opportunity.

Then again, had she done so he would be dead right now.

He wanted to believe her. She had, in fact, saved his life. For that, he owed her his allegiance, at least temporarily.

It had been a very long time since he had allowed anyone close enough to make him wish for things he did not have. He wanted for little and the idea of wanting more seemed far too selfish. Yet he could not push aside this need she had awakened.

If she turned out to be his enemy, he could not say that he would not be disappointed. For now, he would give her the benefit of the doubt. Perhaps she was an adventurer. He spent so little time with others that he was not at all sure his judgment was adequately balanced. Once thing was certain—American women were very different from those of his homeland. Maybe if he had bothered with a social life, he would not be so quick to jump to conclusions regarding a strong, determined woman.

A sound in the distance, a snap or crack, jerked his attention from his foolish thoughts. With the sunrise came a satisfied silence from nature. The insects no longer trilled and the frogs had stopped their deep croaking. There was only the sound of the leaves stirring when the breeze roused them and the occasional splashing of water as the natives to the park went about their morning rituals of survival.

But this sound had not been a noise created by nature.

"Renee," he whispered against her soft hair.

She sat up instantly and looked around.

He touched a finger to his lips.

Another noise grazed his senses, this one slightly closer.

Her eyes widened with recognition. She heard the intrusion as well.

Getting up without making noise was not an easy feat, but necessary all the same. He checked the area where they had spent the night, plumping and straightening the flora to ensure it did not draw attention. After surveying the area around them for the most effective possible route of escape, he took her hand and started the painstaking movement away from the approaching trouble. Waiting to see if a park ranger was simply making his rounds this morning would be too much of a risk. He hastened his step as soon as it appeared safe to do so.

The deeper they moved into the park, the thicker the vegetation. The path grew more narrow as the swamp closed in on dry land. He couldn't be certain that continuing in this direction was safe or logical.

He stopped. She stayed close behind him and did not ask questions. The slightest sound could give away their location. He listened long enough for his heart rate to return to normal and to conclude that trouble had not picked up their trail.

Pushing onward could prove detrimental if help was close by. The thicket of mangrove trees to his right might provide a temporary hiding place until he could determine whether the approaching party was help or trouble. A ranger would be able to radio for help and could direct them to safety much more quickly than he could hope to do with the aid of a compass or map.

He weaved his way through the dense foliage until he reached the thicket he had spotted. The vegetation and soft soil that abutted the trees provided the perfect haven for snakes and alligators. He had no choice but to proceed cautiously and wish for the best.

She stalled.

He looked back, couldn't risk speaking to her. He could only urge her with his eyes and hope she would understand that they had no other choice.

Movement twenty or so meters back the way they had come propelled her into action. She gingerly took the same path he had.

Once stationed behind the mangroves, he permitted a deep breath. They were close now. The fact that those approaching had started to move so quickly, as if they had suddenly picked up a trail, negated the possibility of a park ranger. A ranger would have no need to rush. He was certain this was trouble.

Renee felt the air flee her lungs when one of Victor's men, whom she'd had the misfortune of bumping into twice already since coming to Florida, came into view. She peered between the twisting throng of branches as he came closer. Behind him were two other men. All were heavily armed. As she watched, the men broke ranks, taking off in different directions.

She was certain that the only reason one of them hadn't already approached their position was that they stood in water about twelve inches deep in the snakiest-looking spot she'd seen so far. No one in his right mind would hide here. She shuddered inwardly as she considered those facts.

Even a brief visual examination of the weapons the three carried made her damned glad that Paul had chosen this spot.

Two of the men had disappeared into the woods on either side of the one progressing in their general direction. This one seemed to be in charge, she'd noticed from their previous encounters.

Her heart bounced against the wall of her chest when he continued to move closer and closer to their hiding place. Paul's arm went around her as if he'd sensed her mounting trepidation.

If they were murdered out here, would their bodies be found before the animals ate their fill? She bit down on her lower lip to stop its annoying trembling. Her life had been threatened before. Bomb threats at the courthouse. Warnings that if she proceeded with a case she would be harmed in some way.

But this was a little different. There were no armed sheriff's deputies standing between her and the possibility of danger. And she didn't have a weapon.

There was only this man. She glanced at him from

the corner of her eye. A man who rarely left his home, an artist who likely had little, if any, defensive or offensive training. And sheer determination.

Victor's hired killer stopped as if he smelled or sensed his prey. Renee froze, her heart staggered. The scumbag was no more than ten or twelve feet from their position. Slowly, he scanned the area.

It was at that precise second that Renee faced one of the toughest challenges of her life. If she survived this first mission that had taken a definite turn for the treacherous, this would be, in her estimation, one of the defining moments of her true courage.

Something slithered through the murky water, curved around her left calf, its cold skin sliding against hers, forcing goose bumps to rise on her body like tiny knots of absolute terror. She clenched her jaw. Didn't dare breathe.

Seeming satisfied, the man moved on. So did the snake or whatever the hell had slinked around her leg.

Renee took a jagged breath, let it go. Still, she didn't dare move. The tiniest sound could bring one or all of Victor's men charging back toward their hiding place.

The urge to look behind her was suddenly overwhelming. What if one of the others had made his way around to come up behind them?

Another glance at Paul and she knew he'd considered that very possibility. With his body positioned at a slight angle, he watched behind them for a time before turning his attention back to the more apparent danger. If she looked past his profile, she could see beyond him, as well.

Endless minutes dragged by. If they moved too soon, one of the thugs might hear them. So they held still.

Her legs, above and beneath the water, had started to itch. The way the slinky fabric of her slacks stuck to her skin only make matters worse. The urge to move back onto dry land was almost unbearable. Mosquitoes were feasting on her, but she didn't dare fan them away or swat at the pesky predators.

Jim Colby would be worried if she didn't call in again soon. Obviously Victor hadn't been caught, since his men were still out looking for Paul.

The possibility that Agent Joseph Gates was working against them made her furious. What had he hoped to gain by being a part of this? Their client, Darla Stewart, believed she could trust him. Her dead brother, the cop, had trusted him. That made Gates the lowest of the low. An accessory to a cop killer…to the man responsible for drugs pouring into their country, tainting their youth…such as her own brother.

God, she needed to check on that situation, as well. For all she knew, a new date of execution could have been set. But he didn't want her involved; she had to let that go. Not your problem, she reminded herself, clenching her jaw to hold back the emotion that rose in her throat.

This was her job. Getting this guy safely out of this damned jungle. Helping to bring down a mass murderer and his accomplices.

Focus. Wait until it was clear and then start moving. Get as far away from these bastards as possible.

Locating a park ranger would be good. He would have supplies at his station and the means to get out of here without further incident. She could definitely use a long, cool drink of water about now. But if Victor's men were anywhere around when that happened, the ranger would end up dead, as would the two of them.

Putting as much distance as possible between them and those lowlifes was imperative.

Paul leaned closer, put his lips to her ear. "Let's go."

Nothing would make her happier than getting out of this swamp, but what if they hadn't waited long enough?

"Shouldn't we wait a little longer?" Her lips were so dry the whisper came out roughly. She moistened her lips and willed her heart to slow its sudden hammering.

"I believe it's safe." He eased out of their hiding place first. He barely made a sloshing sound. She hoped she would be as fortunate.

Holding her breath, she climbed out after him. Hardly a sound. Relief washed over her.

Her leather sandals were sodden. Honestly, she didn't know how they had held together this long.

Looking back at the mucky area where they'd hidden, she shuddered.

Paul took her hand and headed back the way they had come.

He moved faster with every step, still taking care to remain as noiseless as possible. She let him lead for now. As long as they were moving away from the danger, she couldn't say she would have done anything differently.

Not much she passed looked familiar. Since she'd been running for her life when she'd come this way and taking time to notice the landscape had been the last thing on her mind, that wasn't surprising. Then it had become dark and she'd had enough trouble avoiding head-on collisions with trees.

Paul hesitated. To get his bearings, she presumed. She scanned the waist-deep underbrush and dense tree population for anything even remotely familiar.

She would have been okay if she hadn't looked up.

Major mistake.

Never in her life, not even in her grandfather's barn, had she seen such massive spiderwebs. They sprawled from tree to tree.

And then she saw the occupants. Big spiders. Some bigger than others, but all huge in comparison to the ones she'd seen in her lifetime. Yellow-and-black-striped legs. Big bodies with red spots.

Fear curled its way around her chest, squeezing out the last of her breath.

She could deal with snakes if necessary. In fact, there wasn't a lot that scared her.

But she hated spiders.

Paul tugged her forward. She stumbled, blinked, then jerked back to the here and now.

"Don't look at them," he murmured.

Wouldn't help. Not now. She knew they were there.

"We must hurry," he urged softly.

He was right.

She forced her feet back into action, refused to look upward again. She didn't want to know if there were more of them.

A shout somewhere behind them sent a new kind of fear gliding through her veins like ice.

"This way."

Paul dragged her back into the densest part of the wilderness around them. The soil was mucky. She knew what that meant—they were headed into water again.

Snakes. Alligators. Lots of friendly critters. She glanced up and shuddered. And spiders.

The heat had already grown stifling. Unlike her, the tropical vegetation appeared to thrive in the desert-like temperatures. All the muck and water, she reasoned. The combination made for an environment literally swarming with life.

Up ahead, she saw an egret. It appeared to consider their approach at length before deciding that taking flight wasn't necessary. The beauty of the wild orchids momentarily took her mind off the idea of spiders and guys with guns.

Paul headed for dryer land, urging her toward a cluster of trees, pine and another species she didn't readily recognize.

The new hiding place was somewhat more bearable, considering they weren't standing in a foot of water. But she could see a narrow, murky strait not far from where they hid. A turtle lay sunning itself in a spot where the sun somehow managed to cut a path through the reigning trees.

Not far from the turtle was a shape that almost blended in with the vegetation. She strained to see if maybe it was just a decomposing tree trunk. Movement warned her it was no rotting log. Big eyes blinked slowly before the greenish black form slid into the water and moved away. Thankfully, the prehistoric-looking creature glided off in the opposite direction from where she and Paul were hiding.

Alligator.

She wondered where the egret had got off to. Her memory was a little sketchy on the eating habits of gators, but she was fairly sure egrets were on their diet.

She had a feeling that Paul's choice in hiding places had more to do with the enemy's movements than comfort.

He leaned close. "They are expanding their search grid. We are going to have to keep moving."

She'd reasoned as much. She met his gaze, saw

the worry there. The cell phone tucked into her bra reminded her that she had that one option, but turning it on might lead the enemy right to them. Jim had told her not to use it unless it was an emergency. "Which way do you want to go?"

Paul inclined his head in the same direction the gator had taken.

Perfect. That would have been her first choice, gator or no gator.

The mucky ground sucked at her feet, made walking hard, made keeping quiet even harder.

As if the Man Upstairs wanted to make things even more interesting, the wind started to kick up. Distant thunder rumbled.

Minutes later, rain was coming down in sheets. She couldn't see the lightning streak the sky, but she could feel the charge in the air and the accompanying thunder kept her ears ringing.

They walked as long as they could in spite of, and mostly against, the weather. When it became impossible to see, Paul ushered her toward a mass of tall tropical vegetation that bordered another copse of gnarled mangrove trees.

She was soaked to the bone. She leaned against a tree and wiped the rain from her face. The downpour was starting to let up and the shield of the thick canopy where they stood helped considerably.

Paul stood near the edge of the cover, watching to ensure they hadn't been followed.

Somehow they had to get out of here. Finding their way out of this jungle was going to be impossible if they had to keep evading their would-be killers and backtracking. Hanging around here was not going to work for lying low. All Victor's men would have to do to win this chase was bring on the dogs for tracking. She couldn't take the risk that the idea would occur to them.

She had to get Paul out of here.

But she couldn't do that if they had to stay hidden.

Her stomach rumbled and she ignored it. Food was way down the priority list just now. Water, however, was essential. All the more reason to try and spot a ranger's station.

The rain let up enough for them to start moving again. The sooner they were out of here, the better.

She joined him at the outer perimeter of their hiding place. "Do you think we should keep going? Try to find our way out or to a ranger station?"

He nodded. "There has been no indication that my brother's men followed us this way. The rain may have sent them seeking cover."

But their paths could always intersect, she didn't bother mentioning. There was no guarantee, no matter how careful they were, that they wouldn't get caught.

She was well rested, thanks to Paul. If she stayed alert and kept moving, they would make it. All she had to do was stay focused.

"This way." He took her hand as he did each time and tugged her after him.

She didn't resist. She had gotten used to the feel of his roughened palm meshed with hers.

IT WAS NOON.

He wiped his forehead with his arm and stared up at the portion of sky he could see through the trees. The heat had created a sauna effect. His clothes had partially dried, but the sweat slowed the process. They had been walking for hours. He was certain Renee was tired and thirsty, as was he.

He could not determine if they were headed in a useful direction. There had been no other indication that the men sent to find them were close by. That, at least, was good. The more distance between them, the better.

Renee pulled on his hand. "Wait."

Turning to face her, he instinctively performed a quick scan of the area. There appeared to be no trouble. His gaze settled on her.

"What's that?"

He looked in the direction she pointed, then strained to better see what appeared to be a dwelling of some sort. Not very large.

"A ranger's station," she suggested hopefully.

"Perhaps."

He considered the corner of the small building, or what looked like a building, a moment longer.

Judging by the level of the light, whatever it was it seemed to be in or near a clearing.

"You stay here," he said to Renee, "until I have checked the situation."

She shook her head. "No way. I'm going with you."

Arguing would be a waste of time. The determined set of her shoulders and the grim line of her mouth warned him that she was not going to be dissuaded.

As they neared the edge of the clearing, the designation of the small building as a ranger station became visible.

He felt very grateful that they had finally reached assistance.

Beyond the ranger station, the tropical forest gave way to a seemingly endless river of saw grass.

He hesitated, listened. It was very quiet. Too quiet. This concerned him for reasons not readily apparent.

Next to him, she noticed, as well. "Is anyone here?"

"The rangers have certain areas to oversee," he offered, as much to convince himself as to convince her, keeping his voice low. "Perhaps this one is out making those rounds."

He told himself that was the case, but there was something about how deserted everything was that did not feel right. His instincts were vibrating with warning.

"Maybe there's water."

She pushed ahead of him, and he hurried to slow her.

"We should proceed with caution."

She stared at him for a moment, and something like trust flashed in her eyes. "You're right."

This understanding or trust softened him, made him feel an even stronger need to protect her. He took her hand and she let him, as before, but this time the accompanying feelings were stronger, deeper. Foolishly he wondered if she felt this connection, as well.

Most likely not.

Together they eased closer to the building. He rounded the corner first and moved to the only door. She was close behind.

The door was not locked. Inside, he found what he had expected—a desk, shelves and cabinets.

But no park ranger.

And no radio.

Renee checked the desk, the shelves and cabinets. "Shouldn't there be a radio?"

He looked around again himself, double-checked the places they had both already considered. "Perhaps the radios are portable and the rangers carry them." This was very disappointing.

"At least there's water." She gathered pouches of water and packets of food from the supply cabinet. She studied the available offerings. "Looks similar to the field rations the military use."

Since they had no choice but to wait for the ranger to return, satisfying their hunger and thirst would be beneficial in the event walking out of here was still necessary. He tore open one corner of a water pouch as per the instructions and passed the pouch to Renee, then opened one for himself. Seated on the desk, they ate the food from the foil packets without conversation. He was certain she was as tired and hungry as he was, which prevented the usual pleasantries.

"How long do you think it'll be before the ranger returns?" she asked. "We could stay here until then. Maybe avoid running into trouble again."

He could not speculate with any accuracy on when the ranger would return. Since the building had been unlocked and food supplies were available, he felt sure someone had been there that day. Why would he leave the door unlocked? The policy didn't seem like a very good one to him, but he wasn't certain of the usual protocol.

"I would not be able to guess under the circumstances." He considered her second question. "We can stay here as long as it feels safe."

She stood, gathered and discarded the empty food and water containers before settling her gaze back on him. "Under what circumstances?"

Sharing his concerns would only make her more uncomfortable, but she had a right to know. "The door was left unlocked. We have been here nearly an hour and no one has returned."

She walked to the window and stared out. "That's what I thought." She turned back to look at him then. "Either the ranger who mans this station is missing in action, or he didn't show up today. In which case, I have to wonder who unlocked the door."

He understood what she was thinking. His brother's men may have been here already, or possibly they had run into the ranger while tracking their prey.

The lock and chain on the desk suggested that the small building was usually locked and that a key had been used to unlock it. Since the place had not been left torn apart, he would assume Victor's men had not been here, or if they had, they had not been inside for more than a quick check to determine if anyone was hidden here.

Renee stood by the window, staring out into the treacherous natural beauty. He set his concerns aside momentarily so that he could admire her. It was a selfish indulgence, but he was weary and in need of inspiration. The ivory-colored slacks were soiled and wrinkled, but they did not detract from her appeal. Her hair was a wild mass but that only made him long to thread his fingers there and feel its silky softness.

"How did the ranger get here?" She swiveled toward him. "You suppose he walked?"

He tugged his thoughts back to less precarious emotional territory and considered the acres of saw grass. "Airboat, perhaps."

She shrugged. "But where is the boat?"

He saw her point. "He could be out on a rescue mission. He may have left in a hurry and forgotten to lock up."

"So we continue to wait?"

He flared his hands. "Unless you would prefer to take our chances out there." He nodded to the wilderness beyond this small shelter. "The ranger will return eventually." If he is able, he added silently.

She regarded his suggestion a moment. "There's food and water here. It's dry." She glanced around the room. "No spiders."

He smiled. "Agreed."

"I vote we stay here. Someone's bound to show up sooner or later," she said resolutely.

"Then we stay."

She walked over to the supply cabinet. "There's toilet paper in here. I think I'll take a walk."

He got to his feet. "We should stay together."

Her hands went up Stop-sign fashion. "Sorry. Not for this."

Before he could argue the point, she walked out the door. If she needed privacy, he could understand that, but he didn't like the idea of allowing her out of his sight.

Two minutes.

If she did not return in two minutes, he mentally ticked off the seconds, he was going after her.

Chapter Ten

Renee surveyed the area she'd chosen once more.

Locating a spot that provided adequate privacy wasn't a problem. She took care of necessary business as quickly as possible, her senses alert to every sound, every movement.

The rain had helped considerably in losing those guys. But how long would their good fortune last? Lying low in the ranger's station could work for a while, but staying in one spot was dicey business.

She glanced around before stepping from the shielding bushes. Clear. The sooner she was back inside with Paul, the safer she would feel.

But first she had to try and get through to Jim again. He'd told her to lie low as long as possible. This seemed like as good a place as any, but she couldn't put off checking in any longer.

She turned on the phone. No service. Damn it. Shutting it off, she shoved it back into her bra and glanced around to make sure it was still clear. When she started forward again something on the ground at the edge of a thicket of dense undergrowth snagged her attention.

She crouched down, stared intently at what appeared to be part of a flashlight. Easing closer, she reached out to touch it.

Hard, plastic. She grasped the yellow surface with her finger tips and dragged it toward her. Definitely a flashlight, but it was stuck...or something.

She pulled a little harder. The flashlight cleared the bushes along with the hand still gripping it.

Renee toppled backward. Clamped her hands over her mouth a split second before a scream escaped.

Her heart pounding mercilessly, she stared at the flashlight and hand. The hand was attached to an arm that disappeared into the bushes.

Don't scream, she commanded herself as she lowered her hands from her mouth. *Don't scream.*

Her arms and legs shaking so badly she could hardly organize her movements, she crept closer to the clump of bushes. She parted the branches and took a look.

Male.

Lying face down.

Uniform.

Definitely dead.

Struggling to control her breathing, she touched the man's hand, the one closest to her and still clasped around the flashlight.

Cold. Stiff. Rigor mortis was already present in the extremities. He'd been dead several hours.

As a woman, she wanted to run back to the ranger station as fast as she could. The logical, trained former prosecutor wanted to determine his identity without further contamination to the crime scene.

She should go get Paul.

Chewing her lower lip, she looked toward the station. That would only waste time.

Just do it. She reached into the back pocket of the dead man's trousers and withdrew his wallet.

Breathing slow and deep through her nose to control the roiling in her stomach, she searched until she found what she needed. Driver's license. Dennis Frisk of Marathon, Florida.

She replaced the wallet and wiped her hands on the legs of her pants. Okay.

She jerked her head up at the sound of foliage rustling.

Someone or something was coming.

She scooted behind the bushes concealing the dead man and willed her lungs to hold the air inside.

Paul's profile came into view.

She let go a breath of relief, then stood.

"You okay?" he asked, not coming any closer.

"I…I think I found the park ranger."

Paul was at her side before her brain acknowledged that he'd moved.

She crouched next to him as he squatted down to

take a look. He touched the man's neck to check his carotid artery. She noticed the strange angle of his head then. Whoever had killed him had done so up close and personally by snapping his neck.

A shudder quaked through her.

Paul started to turn the man over.

"What're you doing?" She grabbed his arm to stop him. "This is a crime scene." She was certain he realized that, but apparently he didn't comprehend the rules that went along with that designation. And why would he? she realized too late to take back the words.

His gaze collided with hers. "Looking for a radio or cell phone."

Oh. She should have thought of that. She also should have thought of how he might view her resolve not to violate a crime scene. Not exactly something a regular civilian would think of in a situation like this. Maybe he would assume she'd been watching too many crime scene dramas on television. The fact that she had checked the victim's wallet had been instinct.

And he was right about one thing. They needed help. A radio or phone that actually got service out here would make life a lot easier. Even as an officer of the court, she recognized that end would certainly be a legitimate reason to take the risk of breaching a crime scene. The idea that he might find her ability to be this close to a dead guy without falling apart unusual had her taking steps to undo that image.

She looked away as if the sight were far too gruesome to endure.

Paul exhaled a heavy breath. "Let's go back inside."

She met his gaze and nodded. He pulled the flashlight loose, in case they needed it, she supposed, then offered his free hand to her.

She placed her hand in his and allowed him to assist her to her feet.

This ranger's death couldn't have been coincidence. The men looking for them had done this. She was certain. This was the way she and Paul would end up if they didn't get out of here first.

Inside the small station, she hugged her arms around herself and paced. How the hell could they get out of here? Clearly, lying low here was not a good idea. They had no idea which way to go. There were at least three men out there searching for them.

They were screwed if she didn't get her act together and come up with a new plan.

She should have a better handle on the situation. Think. Her frustration gave way to determination. She had to look at this like a trial. When the case started to crumble, you backed up and regrouped. Revised and rerouted.

Standing around here wondering if they would be rescued or murdered was not the right course of action. She turned her attention to her companion, who seemed to be studying a map.

"We should find our way out of here before it gets dark," she announced.

Paul glanced up. "I agree. I think I've located our position on this map."

"Excellent."

She went back to the supply cabinet and grabbed a couple of packets of water and joined him at the desk. She handed the water pouches to him. "Put one in each pocket. I don't have any pockets or I'd do it."

He did as she suggested, then pointed to the map. "We are here," he said in that vaguely accented voice that made her shiver with something that definitely wasn't fear. "We need to reach this location." He pointed to another spot on the map. "There is a lodge and a café. Perhaps we can find transportation there."

Sounded like a plan.

"Can you get us there?" As long as he thought his help was crucial to their survival, chances were he'd stay close to her. She needed him to believe they were in this together. They were, to a degree. He just didn't need to know why she was involved. His co-operation was essential. The other side of that was the idea that she wanted him close…maybe more than she wanted to admit.

He looked at the map again, then at her. "I believe so." He tucked the flashlight into the back pocket of his jeans. "It's quite a distance. We might not make it before dark."

She nodded her understanding. "We'll give it our best shot."

Outside, she hesitated. Any cop worth his salt would likely argue her reasoning, but she just couldn't walk away like this. It might be hours before Frisk was found. He'd most likely been murdered early in his shift, but who knew what time his relief would come. "We should move his body inside." It was a miracle the carnivores hadn't been after him already.

"You keep watch. I will move the body."

He'd get no argument from her. She was happy to allow her companion to play the "guy" on that score.

Once Frisk's body was in the station, they headed back into the heart of the forest with Paul leading. He'd studied the map. The sun was still high in the sky; the time was maybe two or two-thirty. That left about four or four and a half hours until dark.

They had to move fast. She did not want to spend another night out here with Victor's men tromping around after them.

THEY FOUND THE LODGE shortly after dusk.

If she hadn't been so exhausted, she would have thrown her arms around Paul and kissed him. She told herself that it was nothing more than gratitude, but that was a lie. He'd done a great job of leading them out of the wilderness. It might have taken her twice as long. Working together as a team had proven much more useful than allowing him to know that, for now, he was ultimately her hostage. She didn't need a weapon or threats to keep him close, cultivating his trust had worked far better.

Until they had Victor Reyes in custody, Paul was their ace in the hole. But he didn't need to know that. The instant he realized what she was up to, he would likely bolt. She didn't believe for an instant that he would want to help his brother in any way. But she doubted that he would choose this route to stop him. The image of the two of them battling to the death made her shudder inwardly.

They remained in the edge of the woods and watched before moving forward.

"Three of the rooms are occupied."

Looked that way to her, too. The other rooms were dark, with no vehicles parked in the designated slots. "I count ten vehicles total. The others must be patrons of the café."

"Or employees."

She agreed. No black SUV, but that didn't mean Victor's men weren't around. There could be a whole lot more than the three she'd met so far. She couldn't be sure what other makes of vehicles they might have at their disposal.

Only one way to find out.

One of them had to go in. Putting him at that kind of risk was out of the question.

It had to be her.

Using her fingers as a comb, she attempted to tame her hair. She smoothed her blouse as best she could. Her clothes were dry, if not clean. "I'm going in."

He put a hand on her arm. "No. I'll go in."

She shook her head. "If any of his men are hanging around in there they might not recognize me, but they'll damned sure know you." Paul and Victor were practically twins; neither could deny the family tie.

"No." Paul's grip tightened.

His protectiveness made her feel warm inside even as it annoyed her. She could get used to the whole I'll-take-care-of-you mentality…to a degree, she amended. But now wasn't the time. "I'll be okay." She gently tugged her arm free of his hand. "Just stay out of sight until I check out the situation."

"Three minutes," he warned. "If you are not back in three minutes, I will come for you."

"Give me five, okay?" Since he didn't have a watch, she wasn't sure how he intended to accurately measure the time. Better a little more than not enough.

He didn't agree, but he didn't argue, either.

He needn't have worried. She wasn't about to allow him out of her sight any longer than absolutely necessary.

At the entrance to the restaurant, she smoothed her hand over her hair once more and took a deep, bolstering breath. She looked like hell, but there wasn't a lot she could do about it.

Now or never.

She opened the door and stepped inside. The scents of grilled and fried foods had her stomach grumbling. Thankfully there was no hostess to waylay her. A dozen tables with Formica tops and chairs sporting yellowed white vinyl seats filled the black-and-white-tiled dining area. A buffet-style bar took up a good portion of one side of the room. A couple of patrons perused the selections, plates in hand. Double doors led into the kitchen.

The cashier was busy ringing up a customer. Renee walked over to the counter and picked up a menu. She peered over the menu instead of at it so that she could survey the occupants of each table. No one that looked familiar to her. Most were families. Husband, wife and children. She doubted any of Victor's henchmen would be traveling with their families. If the world were lucky, those guys wouldn't be procreating.

"Did you want to place a take-out order?"

Renee laid the menu aside and produced a smile. Just when she'd decided she didn't have a plan, inspiration struck.

"No. I'm here to see my cousin." She gestured to the busboy who was clearing a table across the room. "Thanks anyway."

The cashier shrugged and turned her attention to wiping the counter.

Renee wet her chapped lips and considered a moment what she intended to say to the young guy she'd claimed was her cousin. Tall, skinny, blond hair, good tan and old enough to drive. He didn't look up until she'd walked all the way over to the table where he worked. "Hi." She hung on to her smile. "Looks slow around here tonight."

He surveyed the room. "You shoulda been here earlier. It was a madhouse."

This was a whole hell of a lot harder without a gun. She had no choice but to rely on her powers of persuasion. At least in the courtroom she had a captive audience. It wasn't like the jury was going to tell her to get lost or run out on her.

"Look," she said, finally latching onto an idea that didn't include the phrase *help me out or I might just end up dead,* "I hate to bother you while you're working, but my car won't start. I think the battery's dead. I was wondering if you'd give me a jump."

A frown tugged at his expression as he looked around at the four or five tables that needed to be cleared. Evidently he'd been right. She'd gotten here right after the rush.

"Please," she urged. "I really could use your help."

He sighed. "Okay. Where's your car? I'm out back."

"I'm right out front."

"Come on." He grabbed the shallow tub of dirty dishes. "I have to get my keys."

"Thanks. I really appreciate it."

Renee followed him through the kitchen. Two

cooks and a dishwasher glanced up, but didn't bother looking for more than a second or two.

Her busboy settled his load onto the stainless steel counter next to the guy washing dishes by hand. "I'll be right back."

"You shouldn't be taking a smoke break until all those tables are bused," the dishwasher groused. "You get behind, I get behind."

The busboy flipped him off as he grabbed his keys from the table by the rear exit. The dishwasher rolled his eyes and dived back into his work. Renee kept that stupid smile tacked in place as she followed the young man out the back door. She hoped the dishwasher didn't get suspicious and come out to see what they were up to.

"He's a jerk," the busboy said, then motioned to the blue pickup truck that easily fit into the category of antique. "That's mine. Hop in. We'll drive around to where your car is parked." He shot her a smile. "My name's Kenny, by the way."

"Renee," she returned as she climbed into the passenger seat as he slid behind the wheel. "You live around here?"

"Florida City," he said as he lit up a smoke and then, as if out of consideration for her, he rolled down his window. "How 'bout you?"

She shook her head. "Just visiting. I took a trip in the park that ended badly."

He started the engine and pulled the gearshift into

Reverse as he looked her up and down. "You get lost out there?"

She started to lie, but decided that since she undoubtedly looked like that was exactly what had happened she might as well 'fess up. "Yeah. Spending the night in a swamp wasn't exactly how I pictured this vacation going," she fibbed. "I don't think I'll be coming back anytime soon."

He grinned. "Folks get lost all the time. They still come back."

Not me, she didn't bother saying. She'd seen all the nature she cared to for a long time to come. Give her the streets of Chicago anytime. She didn't have a problem with danger, but she'd take the threat of thugs in city alleys over alligators in the wilderness any day.

He drove around the end of the building and braked. "Which one's yours?" He surveyed the vehicles in the main parking area.

Now came the tricky part. "I was wondering—" Surely they wouldn't fire him if he drove her and Paul into town. She was just desperate enough to ask anyway. It was either that or ask to borrow his truck. She doubted the latter would go over very well.

A big black SUV rolled up to the front of the café and parked.

For three full seconds, her mind refused to register what her eyes saw. Then the two men whose faces were permanently burned on several of her brain cells got out of the vehicle and she was forced to acknowledge that it was really them.

Which put a totally different spin on things.

"Hey, Renee, which car is yours?" the driver griped. "I have to get back in there or my uncle'll be big-time mad."

So much for the power of persuasion. Her attention turned back to the driver. "What did you say your name was?"

His frown deepened. "Kenny."

"Look, Kenny." She watched the two men enter the café. Evidently the third man was dead, lost or in another vehicle. "Those guys who just went inside are after me." Her gaze locked with his. "They're really bad dudes. I need to get out of here." Now for the possible deal breaker. "I need to borrow your truck."

At his confused look, she added, "I'll leave it parked in town. You can pick it up tomorrow."

He laughed, the sound lacked any humor. "You're joking, right?"

"Sorry. No."

His jaw slackened in surprise, but then he said, "Look, this isn't really my truck. I could get in big trouble if my dad finds out."

She stared straight into his eyes and told him the truth. "I could get dead."

"Get out of the truck," a deep, Latin-influenced voice rumbled.

Renee's gaze shot past the busboy to the man who jerked the driver's side door open.

"Get out," Paul reiterated in case the kid didn't get it the first time.

"What the hell's going on here?" Kenny turned to her. At her shrug, he demanded, "Are you two for real?"

"Just let us borrow your truck, Kenny," she urged, "and everything will be fine."

Kenny shoved the gearshift into Park, and got out. Paul climbed in behind the wheel and jammed the transmission into Drive once more. He jammed his foot against the accelerator and the vehicle rocketed forward.

"That was totally unnecessary," she grumbled as she watched Kenny stalk back off toward the rear of the building. If he went in there and announced what had just happened, which he most likely would, those guys would be out here on their tail so fast. Damn. They should have just brought the kid with them. But then he might have got hurt.

"You weren't having such good luck convincing the young man to cooperate."

She didn't argue with him. She kept her attention on the front of the café. No sign of Victor's men yet. She didn't know if the head start they were gaining would be enough, but it was something.

The café was almost out of sight when the door flew open and two men burst out.

"Damn it!"

"They're coming?"

"They're coming." There was no way in hell they were going to outrun these guys in this old truck.

"Turn off somewhere!"

"What?" Paul demanded.

"Turn. Left. Right. It doesn't matter. Just turn!"

Paul made a sharp left turn. Tires squealed and Renee barely stayed in her seat.

The truck bumped over the rougher gravel side road.

"Turn off the headlights," she urged. "Hurry!"

Paul shut off the lights. He drove a short distance, parked and cut the engine.

They turned simultaneously to watch the main road they'd abandoned in such a hurry.

One minute turned into two, then three.

If they were lucky the bastards would drive right on by. But if they slowed…if they used a spotlight or something to look…they were done for.

The black SUV roared past.

Renee breathed a major sigh of relief.

"Good call," Paul said softly.

"We should just sit tight for a while." She relaxed into the seat.

He leaned his head back and exhaled loudly. "Another good call."

The night sounds of the Everglades invaded the interior of the truck. The air was thick with humidity.

She turned toward the man behind the wheel. She couldn't really see him, just the outline of his profile. But she didn't need to see. She had memorized the way he looked, the way his lips moved when he spoke. Such a kind, restrained man. How could he be the brother to such a violent, evil being?

"You have something to say?"

The sound of his voice made her shiver. She shifted in her seat, faced forward. This was not the time to feel this damned attraction. As if she had any control over how her body reacted to the sound of the man's voice.

"No…I'm just trying to figure out where we go from here." At least that was what she should be doing.

"He will not stop."

She turned toward him once more. Part of her wanted to tell him that she knew how this kind of betrayal felt. Having one's brother play the part of deceiver made the devastation all the worse. She could not think about that right now. It was a miracle she and Paul were both still alive. Getting bogged down in her past would not promote staying that way.

She had to stay focused on the present.

"I know," she agreed, her own voice as somber as his had been. Victor would not give up until one of them, he or Paul, was dead.

"Who are you, Renee Parsons?"

She could lie some more. Maintain her cover until she could contact Jim Colby and bring Paul to safety. But that wouldn't change a thing. Without Victor, all of this would be for nothing. And there was no guarantee that if Paul knew the truth, particularly the part about how she'd kept the truth from him, that he would cooperate.

She needed him to finish this.

There was no point in adding more lies to the growing mass already mounting between them. They were way past that.

Her best bet—until she could come up with a better plan—was to distract him.

Once the notion was born, there was no stopping putting thought into action. She leaned toward him, kissed his jaw, just the lightest brushing of her lips against that warm skin. The quivering sensations that bombarded her stole her breath. The fingers of his right hand fisted in her hair before she could draw away. He pulled her closer so that he could claim her mouth with his. She opened at his touch, parted her lips for his complete possession.

His touch was tender yet thorough. This was a slow, utter indulgence of the senses. His lips felt firm and somehow soft and smooth. Slowly, his left hand moved up over her torso to settle on her breast. She whimpered at this touch, wanted to do something with her hands, as well. Her fingers splayed on his chiseled jaw, delved into his silky hair. She wanted to be closer. Needed to mesh more fully with him. An urgency swam through her blood, making her ache for more than just this kiss. She wanted him to hold her in his arms as he'd done last night.

His tongue delved into her mouth, slid over places she had never known to be so sensitive before. She trembled, felt the tension begin to build. Impossible. They were still fully dressed. He couldn't bring her to this place with just a kiss.

And yet here she was. Close to the edge.

She moaned, panted with the rising need. She wanted more than this. She wanted…

Victor's killers could come back at any second.

Renee pulled free of his possessive kiss.

She reminded herself to think about what the hell she was doing.

"We're not safe out in the open like this."

His hesitation had her heart lunging into her throat. What if he insisted on questioning her further? What if…

"Where shall we go?"

The strain in his voice could be about his own desires…or it could be a thinning of his patience. No time to dwell on that.

"We could go back to my hotel. They won't expect us to risk going back there."

"And then?"

He was looking at her. There wasn't enough light for her to see his eyes, only the shadow of his face.

But he was looking straight at her. He wanted answers. He deserved answers.

Just not right now.

"Then we'll figure this out."

Chapter Eleven

"It doesn't look good, Mr. Johnson."

Sam Johnson regarded DEA Agent Joseph Gates for a moment before he responded. "There's no blood. No sign of a struggle. Nothing." Sam stared out the wall of windows at the fantastic view of the ocean that served as a permanent backdrop to the property of Paul Reyes. "It's as if no one was ever here." His gaze met that of Agent Gates again. "Except for the fact that her rental car is out front. I find that disturbing, Agent."

Gates nodded. "As do I, but you have to understand, Johnson, this is Victor's M.O."

Sam had gone to Renee Vaughn's hotel first thing that morning and found nothing. The woman was just as neat with her toiletries as she was with her paperwork at the office. Then he'd checked out this place. The home of Paul Reyes was clean.

Almost as if someone had wiped every damned surface to ensure nothing would be found. Vaughn had told Colby that the DEA had torn the place apart. There was absolutely no indication the house had been searched. In Sam's experience, when a place was this clean, it probably had been wiped. The motive in this case eluded him. If Victor was in-country, why? Why take the risk? What was he after? Better yet, what or who was after him?

And if Vaughn was certain that the man traipsing through the Florida Everglades with her was Paul Reyes, then who the hell was this guy?

Sam leveled his attention on the other man in the room—the one claiming to be Paul Reyes. "How many men usually accompany Victor?" he asked. According to what Vaughn had told Colby, two had escorted them from this location.

"A minimum of two."

"Mr. Reyes, are you sure there was nothing taken from your home? No money, passport, nothing?" Sam didn't like this guy. Maybe because he had reason to believe he was lying; Vaughn's word counted, in his opinion. Whatever the case, he just didn't care for the jerk.

The man claiming to be Paul Reyes had agreed to cooperate after reporting a run-in with his brother's men, who had abducted Renee Vaughn. He had barely gotten away.

Reyes moved his head slowly from side to side.

"I'm afraid, Mr. Johnson, that my brother is quite self-sufficient. I would have nothing of consequence to him. We have not spoken in many years."

"Why do you suppose he came here looking for you?" This was the part that stuck in Sam's craw. Victor Reyes stayed clear of American territory for fear of being arrested. Why would he show up at his brother's Key Largo residence out of the blue, so to speak? Why kidnap Vaughn? How could he have known who she was or that she was here to lay a trap for him?

According to Vaughn, Victor was attempting to assume Paul's identity, thus allowing Paul to take the fall for his crimes. Made sense, if it were doable. The two could pass for twins, and neither had a lot of paper on who he was. Lack of dental records, finger-prints, et cetera, left the possibilities wide open.

"I can only assume that he was warned that some-one had been sent here to use me against him. Per-haps he intended to not only stop your friend, but also to ensure I could no longer be a trifle to him. Or perhaps he believed Ms. Vaughn was someone im-portant to me, and he wants to use her to lure me into some sort of trap. I can only guess."

To Sam's way of thinking, the identity theft was the most likely scenario, but even it had major holes in the timing and success possibilities. Men like Victor Reyes simply didn't act without covering all the bases. Playing it safe was how he'd avoided prosecution all these years. Seemed a little strange for him to deviate from that strategy now. "How do you suppose he learned that Vaughn wasn't Renee Parsons?" Sam proposed. "There was only one person who knew about this operation besides my people." He turned to Gates, his expression openly accusing. "Isn't that right, Agent Gates?"

The agent's gaze narrowed. "Are you accusing me of something, Mr. Johnson?"

Sam shrugged. "I haven't decided yet."

"I am sorry, Mr. Johnson," Reyes said, shattering the tension suddenly pushing the air out of the room. "I have no idea how my brother knew anything. Personally, I was completely fooled by Renee." He looked to Gates and then back to Sam. "I was under the impression that she was an art buyer from Los Angeles, just as she said."

Maybe so. "You have no hired help?" Sam wanted to know. "No one who can confirm your activities during the past forty-eight hours? Or who could report those activities to your brother?"

Reyes lifted his expensively clad shoulders and allowed them to fall once more. "You may ask Mallory Rogers, the art gallery owner with whom I do business, or any of my neighbors. I have no staff and I seldom leave my home, other than for occasional gallery showings."

"No shopping?" Sam pried. "No dates?" The idea that he insisted he rarely left the home didn't quite sit right with Sam. This guy had that whole macho attitude going on, from the clothes to the way he held himself—shoulders back, feet wide apart, chin lifted arrogantly. Someone who was spending some major bucks. Sam had worked around the celebrities in the Los Angeles area long enough to recognize designer rags. Not to mention the car and the furnishings. Didn't act like any recluse Sam had ever encountered.

"All my needs are brought here to me," Reyes insisted. "I have no need for a staff. A service comes in once per week to take care of the housekeeping. I'm never here when they come. As I said, anything I need is delivered right to my door."

Sam cocked his head and eyed him with mounting suspicion. Suspicion he didn't mind sharing with his new pals. "Are your female friends delivered here to you as well?"

"Mr. Johnson," Gates said, his tone reprimanding, "We are very fortunate that Mr. Reyes has agreed to cooperate fully with us. Let's not go out of our way to insult him for no reason."

"Sorry." Sam wasn't. The only thing he felt was more suspicious of the man claiming to be Paul Reyes. Something was off here; he just hadn't put his finger on what it was yet. But he would. Vaughn would have her reasons for believing the man with her was Paul Reyes. Sam's only hesitation was the idea that the real Victor Reyes would have the nerve to stand in the room with the DEA all around him and not even flinch.

But then, the guy was one sick SOB from what he'd read in Reyes's file.

"I hope," Reyes offered with a sincerity Sam couldn't deny visually, "that your friend is safe, Mr. Johnson. My brother is a vicious killer. If I can help you stop him, I would very much like to do so."

Sam needed to touch base with Jim Colby and give him an update, but he had just one more question. "Why the sudden change of heart?" he asked Reyes. "For years, the DEA has attempted to nail your brother. You've never offered to help before. What'd you do, wake up with a conscience this morning?"

Gates shifted with his escalating discomfort at Sam's attitude, but he kept his mouth shut on this one. Sam didn't really care if Gates liked him or not. He wasn't here to make friends.

For three tension-filled beats, he wasn't sure the man would respond to his blatantly skeptical question about his moral standards.

"I do not agree with Victor's way of life," Reyes said with equal bluntness, "but he is my brother. However, when his men came into my home and tried to kill me, he crossed the line. He is no longer my brother."

Sam nodded. He understood perfectly. If Gates hadn't liked his line of questioning thus far, he sure as hell wasn't going to like this. "So, you didn't care how many kids he was killing with his drugs, but the minute he endangered you, you're happy to come forward. Do I have that straight?"

"Johnson," Gates warned.

Reyes held up a hand. "It is all right, Agent. I understand Mr. Johnson's meaning perfectly. Yes, I suppose I loved my brother more than I should have. That is my mistake. I shall carry that burden with me for the rest of my life. But now I am prepared to do the right thing. I will help you in whatever way possible. Let me do this, Mr. Johnson, and perhaps the Father in Heaven will have mercy on my soul."

Sam searched his face, his eyes. Maybe this guy was on the up-and-up. Maybe not. Sam would reserve judgment until he had the lowdown from Vaughn. Whatever the case turned out to be, he'd made his point. "I was out of line," he admitted to get back in the good graces of the agent glaring at him. Sam pulled his cell phone from his pocket. "I have to check in with my office." He started to turn away, but hesitated. "There is one other thing, Mr. Reyes, that might be helpful to my investigation."

"Whatever I can do," Reyes repeated.

"Since you and your brother look so much alike and neither of you have ever been printed for any reason, it would be great if we could dig up some identifying physical trait that would confirm who's who. Or better yet, medical or dental records. Can you help with that?"

Gates exhaled his frustration. "Now you're accusing Mr. Reyes of lying about who he is," he suggested.

Sam smiled. "You have to admit, that's about the only way any of us are ever going to know for sure."

"He is right," Reyes agreed. "This must be settled once and for all. Perhaps I can assist you with this matter. You are correct, my brother and I are very similar from the outside. But there are differences."

"I'll need more than just your word," Sam challenged.

Gates interrupted, "You know we don't have any medical or dental records on the Reyes brothers."

"Actually," Reyes interjected, "I may have something useful."

Tension rippled through Sam. How convenient.

"What're you talking about, Paul?" Gates wanted to know, evidently as surprised to hear this as Sam.

"I may have indisputable proof," Reyes assured, then he smiled. "You will see. I am Paul Reyes. If your friend is still alive, and I pray that she is, it is most definitely my brother Victor who is with her."

Chapter Twelve

Time Unknown

What was she hiding from him?

Paul looked both ways before pulling out onto the long deserted stretch of highway.

He was still grappling with this powerful emotion that had taken him by the throat the instant their lips met. He struggled to focus on driving. Victor's men could decide to turn around and come back at any moment. He had to be prepared.

But he couldn't stop thinking about her.

She sat within arm's reach, the taste of her still on his lips.

Never had he felt such a fierce need to claim a woman. The urge was primal and certainly unreasonable. He knew very little about Renee Parsons, and he suspected that she was not being fully honest with him.

No, he did not suspect, he *knew*.

Logic did not stop him from wanting her so very badly.

Perhaps the insanity that had descended upon his life just over one month ago, combined with running for their lives for the past thirty or more hours, had driven him to this place of ill reason. He could not say for sure.

He released a breath of frustration and tightened his grip on the steering wheel.

For now, survival was of primary importance. His first objective must be to get Renee to a safe place, and then he would do what he already knew he must.

Face Victor.

Otherwise this would never end.

One of them had to die. There was no pretending anymore.

"What is the name of your hotel?" he asked, shattering the suffocating silence.

"The—"

She twisted around in the seat. "Oh, God. It's them."

"What?" He stared at the rearview mirror. Headlights bobbed as a vehicle pulled onto the road from a side road just as they had done not more than five minutes prior.

Even as he watched the vehicle roared closer, the headlights bearing down on them.

"Faster! You have to go faster," she shouted.

He floored the accelerator. The old truck lurched forward.

"Dammit! No signal."

He glanced at her. She held a cell phone in her hand. Where had that come from? The boy? Kenny? Had she found it in this truck?

She reached across his lap. "They're going to ram us. You need to get your seat belt on." She snapped the old-fashioned lap belt into place.

The SUV bumped them before she could get her own snapped around her hips.

Renee slammed into the dash.

He grabbed for her, then swerved to keep from hitting the ditch.

"I'm okay!" She rubbed the side of her head. "Just drive!"

He heard her lap belt snap, and he relaxed a fraction. At least until he glanced at the rearview mirror. "They're coming again!"

He braced against the steering wheel. Renee moved her feet into position on the dash to brace for the crash.

The impact sent the old truck spinning off the road.

Paul tried to control the vehicle, but there was no use.

The truck roared into the underbrush, coming to a rocking halt in the muck.

"Get out!" she shouted as she struggled with her seat belt. "Run!"

He released the latch of his seat belt and shoved the door open.

Doors slamming jerked his attention to the side of the road some twenty meters away.

They were coming.

"Get out, Paul!" she urged. "My door is jammed."

He stumbled out, his feet sinking into water up to his knees. She scrambled out behind him.

"Run!"

Too late.

"Don't move or you're dead."

Renee put her hands up. No need to pretend. They were caught. Better alive and captured, than fleeing and dead.

"Good girl," one of the jerks said as he reached for her.

"Don't touch her," Paul growled.

The sound of a fist connecting with his jaw made Renee's stomach clench.

"Give me your hands," the other scumbag demanded of Paul.

He thrust out his hands, but didn't take his eyes off her. She tried to tell him with her eyes to stay calm, to let them do this, but she wasn't sure he could see the urgency she needed him to. The moonlight was brighter than last night, especially considering they were clear of the trees, but it was still damned dark.

"Let's go."

Her personal scumbag shoved her toward the SUV. She didn't give him any grief. She climbed the slight embankment and headed for the vehicle. Thankfully, Paul did the same.

Renee was loaded into the front passenger seat while Paul was pushed into the back.

"Make one mistake and I'll blow his brains out," the lowlife climbing into the backseat said to her, as if she didn't get the point of the gun jammed into Paul's temple.

They drove back to Key Largo, but didn't go to Paul's house. Instead they went to a house on the low-rent side of the village. Once inside, she and Paul were forced into what might have been a master bedroom. The carpet had seen better days, and there wasn't a stick of furniture. To her supreme relief there was an en suite bath. The windows in both rooms had been boarded up on the inside, and there was nothing in the bathroom except the fixtures.

One of the men patted her down, didn't find anything, and then moved on to Paul.

She'd lost the cell phone in the truck when they crashed, so she didn't have anything for them to find. Neither did Paul.

"What are we doing here?" she demanded when the man was about to leave them in the room.

He hesitated at the door just long enough to look back at her. *"We,"* he said smugly, "are waiting for our next orders. You two are waiting to die."

The door slammed behind him, and a lock was snapped into place.

She took a moment to picture that guy with a bullet between his eyes, then she exhaled as if ridding her body of the foul thought.

"Let's see if we can get each other untied," she said to Paul. He stood very still watching her. She wasn't sure whether he was in shock or had decided that he couldn't trust her. She didn't want him to start asking questions again. At this point, the last thing they needed was doubts between them.

His hands were bound tightly. Too tightly; blood seeped past the ropes around his wrists. Bastards.

She struggled with the first knot until she got it loose. The second one was a bit easier to free. Pretty soon, the nylon rope fell away.

Taking his turn, he worked with the rope binding her until he'd freed her hands.

"Thank you." She rubbed her wrists where the rope had chaffed the skin.

"You're bleeding."

He touched her forehead just above her right eye. She winced.

"Come."

He took her hand as he had several times during their journey through the Everglades and led her into the cramped bathroom. There was no soap or towels, but there was water. As she watched, he ripped off a piece of his shirt and rinsed it over and over, until he was satisfied that it was as clean as it was going to get. Gently, he dabbed at the injury on her forehead.

His face was intent on her, his hand shaking ever so slightly as he worked.

She'd caught a glimpse of herself in the mirror and it was a pretty scary sight. A shower would be great. And clean clothes. But she feared that neither of those things were going to do her any good.

If they didn't get out of here, they were both dead.

"We need bandages." He frowned as he studied the small gash.

She was pretty sure stitches wouldn't be necessary, but a couple of butterfly tapes would be useful. "I'll be fine."

He dropped his hands to his sides. He looked tired and defeated. She wished there was something she could say to lighten the situation, but there wasn't. This was bad. Really bad.

She took the piece of fabric he'd used as a cleaning cloth from him and rinsed it repeatedly. Then she washed his wrists where the rope had torn the skin. She tossed the cloth into the sink and smiled at him. "Now we're both good." It was a lie, but it sounded upbeat.

He settled that dark gaze on hers. "We have a problem, Miss Parsons."

That was the understatement of the decade. "Yes, we definitely have a problem." She glanced around the tiny bathroom. "But for every problem, there's an answer. We just have to find it."

Was that trepidation she saw in his eyes?

"This is a different problem."

A frown furrowed across her brow, making the gash sting. "I don't understand."

"I want very much to make love to you right now, but we have a dilemma." He glanced toward the door leading back into the bedroom. "The timing is not so good."

The heat his admission inspired was nothing short of an inferno. She restrained the need to grab him by the shirt front and show him he wasn't the only one feeling that way. That kiss had set her on the edge and, despite being nabbed by Victor's men, that need still hummed inside her. "You're right, the timing stinks."

For what must have been a full minute or maybe two, the silence expanded between them. She couldn't remember the last time she'd felt this awkward.

He wanted her. Her gaze settled on his face. She wanted him. There was a very good chance that they were going to die in the next few hours.

What the hell.

"Perhaps, I have misread—"

Her next move stalled whatever he'd intended to say. She grabbed him by the shirtfront just as she'd imagined doing and kissed him hard on the lips.

She drew back just far enough to draw in a breath. "The next move is yours," she said when he did nothing but continue to stare at her mouth.

Her challenge prompted him into action. He

peeled her blouse up her body and over her head, then dropped it to the floor. For long seconds he admired her breasts, his breathing growing rapid and uneven.

She gasped when his fingertips grazed the tender flesh at the small of her back as he reached around to lower the zipper of her slacks. She shivered...urged him to hurry.

Paul tried to hurry, but his hands were shaking. She was beautiful. He wanted to see all of her... every shadow and curve. Her skin was so soft and warm. He wanted to taste it. Unable to resist, he pressed his mouth to her shoulder. She quivered, and his body jolted with an answering ripple of pleasure.

He ushered her slacks down her legs, following the fabric downward so that he could lift first one foot and then the other to free her of that encumbrance altogether. He slipped her sandals off, set them aside. While he knelt in front of her, his fingers curled in the lacy fabric of her panties and glided the sensuous material down and off as he had the slacks.

When he stood, before he could unbutton his shirt, she had taken control. She released each button, then pushed the shirt off his shoulders, allowing it to fall to the floor. And then she removed his sneakers and trousers as he had done hers.

When her soft fingers eased his briefs downward, he caught his breath. She pressed a soft kiss against his hip, allowing his erection to nuzzle her shoulder. He shuddered at the incredible vision of her kneeling before him.

He pulled her to her feet and braced her against the wall. He groaned when his body meshed fully with hers. The contrast of her smooth, soft flesh against his hard body was almost unbearable. She reached up to touch his face, her hand trembled. He kissed those trembling fingers and slid his palms around her waist and up her torso to her jutting breasts.

She cried out as he squeezed. His own body jerked with mounting need. He continued to massage and knead those full, lush breasts, her urgent pleas driving him mad. He nuzzled his face in her hair, loved the silkiness of it.

He lifted her, settled her against his waist. The tip of his erection pressed against the damp heat waiting for him. Never before had he wanted anything this much.

"Hurry," she urged.

He shook his head and smiled. "No hurry."

He started at the tip of her nose. He kissed her slowly, thoroughly, learning each new part. Her closed lids. The line of her jaw. The hollow of her throat. That place between her breasts where her heart beat so frantically. And then he suckled each breast until she writhed against him. Her hands moved over his back, her legs wrapped around his waist. She wiggled, tried to usher her bottom down onto him, but he would not allow the full contact...not yet.

Renee couldn't take any more of this. If they were interrupted...she might just die. They had to hurry.

"Stop," she cried.

His head came up, those dark sexy eyes glassy with desire. "You wish me to stop?"

Just looking at him nearly made her come. "No," she said, her voice thick with lust. "I want you inside me. Now."

Those brown, almost black eyes searched hers. She couldn't bear it. She kissed him. Let her lips meld with those firm, full male ones that could work such utter magic.

With one arm around her and using the other for leverage, he lowered her onto that generous erection that had her so hot and bothered.

He flexed his hips, pushed inside her...not all the way but enough to have her moaning with the incredible sensation. He kissed her harder. She shifted her hips, needing more. His body trembled. Finally, he was at the same place as she was, and instinct took over. He thrust deeper.

His lips pulled away from hers just a fraction. "Is that where you want me?"

"Yes." She nipped at his bottom lip.

He moved slowly at first, making her crazy, making her sweat. She pleaded with him to hurry. He ignored those pleas, choosing instead to go painfully slow and ever deeper.

She couldn't hold back any longer. The pleasure cascaded around her, dozens of tiny little explosions. He lunged after her, thrusting faster, harder, until he came apart just as she had.

He pressed his forehead to hers, panting for air. "I am sorry," he said between harsh breaths.

She choked out a laugh. "I'm not. That was amazing!"

He shook his head. "No, I'm sorry I have put you in danger. I swear on my mother's grave that I will do all within my power to protect you."

She caressed his jaw, wished they could make love again. "We'll protect each other, but right now we need to figure a way out of here before our hosts decide it's time to take us to that command performance with death they mentioned."

He kissed her lips one last time before lowering her feet to the floor. The glow shimmering inside her was like nothing she'd ever felt before. Amazing. Amazing and perfect.

After taking care of essentials, Renee wiggled back into her panties and grabbed for her slacks.

Paul reached for his trousers and she touched his back, tracing a six- or seven-inch scar on his lower spine. The scar appeared to be the result of surgery. Not recent, she decided, since the scar looked smooth and any discoloration had long ago diminished. Judging by its location, she guessed it was a spinal injury, but she couldn't be sure. "What's this?"

He thrust one leg into his trousers, then the other. "This is a very old story." He grabbed his shirt. "Are you sure you want to hear it?"

"Yes." She slipped on her blouse. That was the kind of distinguishing physical mark that could confirm who was who. Maybe he hadn't thought of that.

"I was only ten. My brother and I were playing in the barn. I fell from the loft. The damage was more severe than anyone realized, but I was young. The true trouble did not come for a few months. Surgery was necessary, but I was very fortunate that the damage was to a disk very low on my spine."

She stepped into her sandals. "What do you mean you were lucky?" Any spinal damage sounded bad to her. She tugged the straps onto her shoes.

He shrugged those broad shoulders. "If the damage had been here—" he reached around and touched her back just below her shoulder blades "—or higher, the use of my arms or hands might have been affected." He flared his hands. "My work is who I am...why I breathe. I would not be whole without it."

If any doubt had lingered about this man's true identity, that statement obliterated it. He would rather be able to paint than to walk.

"We should hurry," she said, blinking back her

foolish emotion. Man, she'd fallen hard for this guy. She'd definitely be leaving that part out of her report.

There was no way to guess how much time they had. The best way to look at it was that they probably wouldn't have enough, so moving in a hurry was necessary.

Renee studied the way the windows were boarded up. That route would take too long and would make a hell of a lot of racket. She couldn't exactly kick her way through a wall this time. Those scumbags were in this house somewhere.

They needed a distraction.

But first they had to have a strategy.

She had it.

Only he wasn't going to like it.

"It's you they need." She looked him square in the eyes. "I'm expendable."

"Renee—"

"Think about it," she argued. "Victor needs you to complete this scheme of his. I'm not relevant to the outcome. Chances are they'll kill me before we ever leave this house." This was the sticky part. "Unless they have reason not to."

"Fine." He crossed his arms over her chest. "We'll give them reason." His face darkened with worry. "How do we do that?"

She chewed her lower lip, tried to come up with the best way to say this. "The thing is," she started off, "they need me to keep you cooperating, right?"

He nodded, suspicion slipping into his expression.

"If you escape, then they'll need to keep me alive until they have you back where they want you."

He was already moving from side to side before she even finished the statement. "This is not a good plan."

"It's a great plan. They can't kill me if they need me. We have to make them need me."

"And what am I supposed to do when I escape? Assuming we can make this happen."

More dicey territory. "You have to call a friend of mine, Jim Colby. Have him get word to Sam Johnson that you need him."

A frown tugged at his features. "Who are these people?"

She should tell him, but there might not be time.

"I'll have to explain everything later. We can't risk that Victor's time line will preempt ours."

"What shall we do?"

"How long can you hold your breath?"

"A minute? Two?" He looked skeptical, but didn't appear put off by the question.

She quickly ran through the plan she'd hatched. He argued over several points but, in the end, he agreed to do things her way. That he didn't ask any unnecessary questions was a surprise, but he was as aware as she was of the time crunch here.

As Paul got comfortable on the floor, Renee took a couple of deep breaths. Then she screamed.

Screamed a bloodcurdling, at-the-top-of-her-lungs kind of scream. Then she pounded on the locked door for effect.

When the door flew open and one of the men stormed in, his weapon readied for taking down whatever got in his way, she started ranting, "You have to help him! Something's wrong!"

Paul lay on the floor, his body shuddering violently as if he were having seizures.

"What the hell happened?" the scumbag snapped as he shoved his weapon back into his waistband at the small of his back.

"I don't know," Renee wailed as she looked from him to the other man loitering in the door. "He just fell down and then he started shaking. You have to help him!"

Paul suddenly went limp. Renee didn't have to be close to know he'd stopped breathing on cue.

The man kneeling next to Paul leaned closer to see if he was breathing. The man at the door wandered closer to the ongoing drama.

"Is he going to die?" Renee cried.

"He ain't breathing," the guy hovering over Paul said to his cohort.

The other man swore.

As the man leaned close again to try to feel any sign of breath on his jaw, Paul raised his head and snagged the man's ear between his teeth. The man screamed.

The other man moved toward the trouble. Renee

rushed him. Her unexpected move sent him stumbling sideways.

"Don't move!"

The jerk's grip on Renee tightened, but he didn't have time to go for his gun. Paul had the other man's weapon aimed directly at his chest.

"Let her go," Paul snarled.

Dammit. That wasn't the plan. "Just go!" she shouted at him. He wasn't supposed to try and take her with him.

"Back off," he warned the man who still had an iron grip on her arm. "Back off," he repeated. To Renee, he said, "Take his weapon."

She pulled free of the man's loose hold and took his weapon.

"Nothing you do will matter," the man whose ear was bleeding profusely snarled. "He's going to kill you. You know that whatever Victor wants, Victor gets."

Together, Renee and Paul backed out of the room. She quickly snapped the padlock into place.

"We need the keys to the SUV," she said.

He nodded.

The blow came from behind. She didn't see it coming. But she felt it.

Right before the floor flew up to meet her.

Chapter Thirteen

Victor had Renee.

The third man they had encountered in the Everglades, as well as two faces Paul did not recognize, had ambushed them at the house when they had attempted to escape.

Paul had been given his instructions. He had been left at the house where they had been held. Victor's men had provided a wristwatch and a car. Nothing more. One of the men remained to watch him from his vehicle parked on the street. If he attempted to leave early or to stop for anything along the way, Renee would be executed.

Whatever Victor's plan, nothing had been left to chance. Not a single detail had been overlooked. This was the grand finale. There would be an audience, Paul was sure of that. Too much careful preparation had gone into the meeting to assume otherwise.

He drove through the gate to his home…or the place that used to be his home. It did not feel like home now. It felt empty, hollow. He had spent years holed up in this place, pretending he needed no one else. But he had been wrong. He did need someone…he needed Renee.

There were doubts about her. She was certainly no art buyer from L.A. But he knew for certain that she was not involved with his brother's scheming. Whatever her hidden agenda it was not in support of Victor.

If he survived this night, he would know all there was to know about her. That would be his new passion. All else would be secondary.

Paul ascended the steps to the front entrance. The house was utterly quiet.

But the danger was here. He could feel it in the air. Could smell the vile scent of his brother's presence.

Strangely, the front door had been replaced. He reached for the handle, expecting it to be locked, but it was not. He stepped inside the cool, silent interior. It was dark. Somewhere deeper in the house, there was light. He followed the hall until he reached the great room. He hesitated at the door. The only light in the entire house, as far as he could see, was a lamp on the table next to his favored chair inside this room.

In the chair sat his brother.

He made no move to get up. He simply sat there watching, waiting.

"I've been waiting for you."

"Yes, I am aware of that."

It amazed him that the two of them could be so similar on the outside, almost twins, and be polar opposites inside, where it mattered most.

Victor Reyes had no heart.

"You've made quite a mess of all this." Victor shook his head. "Very unlike you, *brother*."

Hearing the term uttered from his vile mouth made Paul shudder.

"I only did what I was forced to do in order to thwart your plan," he countered, enjoying the fury dancing in the other man's eyes. "This is my life and my home. You are not welcome here."

"Ah, but you're wrong." Victor stood. "This is my life...my home."

"Perhaps you have become too intimate with the products you distribute, Victor. I am quite sure you are aware that the authorities will be only too happy to discover you on American soil. You can not hope to pull this off. There are witnesses who know us, dear brother. They will not lie for you."

His brother laughed long and loud. "Foolish, foolish, *brother*. Do you not know me better than that? There are no loose ends. There is no one left."

Anger tightened Paul's jaw. He'd killed them all. Juanita, Eduardo and George. "Do not call me your brother. We are no longer brothers. I should have killed you long ago."

Victor sighed dramatically. "Yes, it would have been so much simpler to have ended this long ago. I tried to kill you when we were mere children, but you refused to die. Our mother watched you closely after that, as did that bitch Juanita, and another chance did not come."

Paul's gut clenched with hatred. On some level he had known that his fall from that barn loft had not been an accident. "You are nothing to me," he sneered, his contempt a palpable force throbbing inside him.

Another of those loud, obnoxious bouts of laughter. "Oh, yes, we are brothers. But in a few minutes there will be only one, and that one will be me." He thumped his chest. "Paul Reyes, the passionate painter who lives such a reclusive life that anyone could take it from him and no one would be the wiser."

"You will not succeed," Paul argued vehemently. "Your only creations are pain and death."

Victor flared his hands and nodded. "That is true. But, alas, the devastating moment to come will force me into an early retirement. How could I possibly continue to create after my only brother attempted to kill me in my own home? The price of *my* paintings will skyrocket."

A new blast of fury detonated inside Paul. "I have

no intention of attempting to kill you," he challenged. "I will never make it so easy for you. You will have to kill me if you want me dead." He held out his hands. "I am unarmed and I refuse to fight you."

Victor's expression turned venomous. "But it is exactly that simple. It is already done. All that is left is the part where you die."

"Then kill me." Paul pounded his chest. "I am here. Why not do it now? If that is your intent. Why bother with this charade."

His brother was right, in part. Without family or friends who knew him well enough to confirm his identity, there really was no other way. Other than dental X rays, and his brother would have ensured that those had been destroyed. He was all too sure of himself not to have taken care of that matter already.

Paul had no idea if there were any old medical records of his back surgery. He had been only a boy. His brother would have covered that, as well. Victor left nothing to chance.

Victor walked slowly, cautiously in Paul's direction, as if he feared for his own safety.

Perplexed, Paul braced for an attack.

His brother threw his arms around him and hugged him as if he were happy to see him, as if none of what had just occurred was real. "Reach into the back of my waistband, *brother*," he said, "and take the weapon."

"What are you doing?" Paul tried to push him away but Victor held on.

"Take it," he commanded.

Paul didn't fight him, but neither did he obey his command. "No," he challenged. "You will not triumph. You are forgetting that I have the scar from the last time you tried to kill me." Remembered pain burned through Paul. As a child, he had believed his brother when Victor claimed the push that had caused him to fall had been an accident, but a part of him had always known the truth. The idea had haunted him. Now he knew why.

"Give me credit, dear brother," Victor said, "I would never forget such an important detail." His hold turned brutal. "Take the gun. Now. Or she dies."

Pain arced through Paul. "You will kill her anyway," he said, the words like daggers twisting in his back. If he went along with Victor, she would die. His only hope was to fight him.

"I'm sure you don't want her to be hurt." His brother smiled at him, the expression sickening. "Do as I say and I will let her live. No one will believe anything she says. She has no proof of what she believes."

"I want to see that she is safe."

As if Victor had been prepared for this very moment, one of his men appeared in the doorway leading into the entry hall. He held Renee in such a way that snapping her neck would require nothing more than a quick jerk. The terror blasted through Paul's veins.

"Take the weapon," Victor murmured for his ears only, "or she dies now."

Paul snatched the weapon from Victor's waistband and stepped back far enough to aim it at the bastard's chest. "Let her go, or I will kill you."

Victor staggered back as if he actually feared for his life. He did not smile but the expression on his face was one of victory. "Goodbye, brother."

RENEE COULDN'T let this happen.

She screamed, "Nooooo!" She jerked free of the hands restraining her and rushed toward Paul.

A shot exploded in the room, shattering glass at the same instant that her body collided with his.

Time seemed to lapse into slow motion as they crashed to the floor together.

The air rushed out of her lungs with the impact.

Instantly, time snapped back and the room was suddenly overrun with armed DEA agents.

Half a dozen voices were shouting, but she didn't hear the words. She was too busy checking to ensure Paul wasn't hit.

"You're okay?" she demanded.

He blinked. Nodded. "Yes."

Strong hands suddenly lifted her to her feet.

Paul was on his feet in a flash, jerking her away from the man who'd pulled her up. He ushered her slightly behind him, protecting her.

"Step away from him, Vaughn," Johnson ordered.

It wasn't until that moment that Renee realized that all those armed agents had their weapons aimed at Paul.

"Get the hell out of my way, Johnson," DEA Agent Joseph Gates ordered. "This man is my prisoner."

"Stand down, Gates," Johnson ordered. His aim steady on Paul, he glanced briefly at Gates. "You tell your men to back off until I have some answers."

The weapon Paul had been holding lay on the floor. There was glass on the floor near one of the French doors. That was when Renee understood that the weapon that had been discharged had been fired from outside…by one of those men. Seven men, all outfitted in full ambush gear like the ones who'd ransacked the house, were bearing down on Paul and Sam Johnson. And her.

"This would have been settled with that one shot if you hadn't interfered," Gates snapped at Johnson. "You interfered with a federal operation. You're going down for that, Johnson."

Gates had shot at Paul? Why?

"What's going on, Johnson?" Renee demanded.

"Step away from him," Johnson repeated. "And we'll talk about this."

"He tried to kill me," Victor Reyes shouted. "You saw him," he said to Renee.

The gun in Paul's hand had been aimed at his brother, but she couldn't say with any certainty what had been going on or why he'd ended up with a weapon. He certainly hadn't had one the last time she saw him.

"Move," Johnson commanded her. To Gates he said, "Keep him out of this until we have a definitive answer."

"What the hell are you talking about?" Renee started to move around Paul, but he stopped her.

"Stay behind me," Paul urged.

"Turn around," Johnson said to Paul, "and lift your shirt. I need to see your back."

This was about the scar.

"What the hell is this, Johnson?" she demanded.

He glanced at Renee. "We have hospital records that prove Victor Reyes had surgery at age eleven. I need to see his back."

Renee shook her head. "He tampered with the records." She shot a look at Victor. "He's using this to fool all of you." This time, she glared at Gates. He had intended to kill Paul—would have, apparently, if Johnson hadn't interfered.

What was to stop him from doing it now?

Moving out of Paul's reach, she darted around in front of him.

"Renee—"

She held up a hand to stop his argument. "Lower your weapon, Johnson." How could they fall for this?

The same way you did.

She had. She'd believed Victor's lies at first. Before she'd met the real man.

"I saw the medical records, Vaughn," her colleague argued. "This has to be sorted out. There is still some question as to which of these guys is Victor Reyes." He shot a nasty look at Gates. "Some of us got a little trigger-happy before the answers could be ferreted out. But we've got it under control now."

"There is no question," Victor roared. "Agent Gates, are you going to allow this? He tried to kill me!"

Renee thought of the scar on the back of the man with whom she had made love. She had promised herself that she would never be fooled by anyone again. That she would never trust anyone again. Not completely.

But she did. She trusted this man. She thought of the story he'd told her about that scar, and she was certain. Absolutely certain.

"He's lying," she said to Johnson as she jerked her head toward the man she knew to be Victor Reyes. "He changed the records. Something. But he is not Paul Reyes. This man—" she gestured to the man at her side "—is Paul Reyes."

Johnson's gaze held hers for two beats. "You're certain about that?"

At that second, she did the one thing she had sworn she would never again do. "Positive."

Johnson lowered his weapon and turned to

Gates. "You heard the woman. You almost killed the wrong man."

"You are dead!"

All eyes shifted to Victor Reyes at the same instant that he snatched a weapon from under his shirt.

Weapons discharged, the explosions deafening.

Renee was suddenly on the floor, with Paul on top of her like a shield.

Victor Reyes lay a few feet away, his open eyes unmoving, a small round hole in the center of his forehead leaking blood.

Renee couldn't move.

Voices.

Frantic movement all around her.

Paul.

"Are you all right?" She searched his face as he attempted to lever his body off hers.

"Yes. Are you hurt?"

"I'm okay." She scrambled out from under him and helped him to his feet. He seemed somehow disoriented. Well, he had just witnessed the execution of his brother. Shock, maybe.

He blinked. "I…"

He collapsed onto the floor.

"Paul!" She dropped to her knees beside him. "Paul!"

Johnson appeared next to her, shouting orders over his shoulder. "Get those paramedics in here now!"

Renee whirled around to see that someone was doing as Johnson had demanded. She hoped like hell that meant the paramedics were on standby somewhere close.

She turned back to Paul. "Was he hit?" she asked Johnson, who was examining him.

He ignored her question and rolled Paul toward her, onto his side to check his back, she presumed, since he leaned over him and took a look. He swore and Renee's heart tumbled toward her stomach.

"What?" she demanded.

Again he ignored her. He gently lowered Paul onto the floor. "Reyes, can you hear me? If you can hear me, talk to me, man."

"I hear you."

His voice sounded weak and thready, but he was still with them. Relief flooded Renee. She leaned close. "Help is on the way, Paul." She struggled to keep the tears out of her voice. "You'll be fine, just hang in there, okay?"

His gaze shifted to hers. She was pretty sure he smiled...his lips tilted ever so slightly, but it was so hard to tell with the tears blurring her vision.

"You still haven't told me who you are," he said thinly, the words crushing her. When she started to explain, he whispered, "Renee...Vaughn?" His face went lax and his eyes closed.

Johnson pushed her out of the way and assumed a position she recognized all too well.

He leaned his cheek close to Paul's face. Paused. Then tilted his head back and commenced CPR.

"Oh, God." She started to shake.

Two paramedics burst into the room and took over.

Johnson dragged her out of the way.

"I don't understand." She watched the paramedics intubate and bag Paul so that air could more easily be forced into his lungs to keep his heart beating. How could this be? There wasn't even that much blood.

"Look at me, Vaughn."

She couldn't take her eyes off Paul as the paramedics prepared to move him.

"Vaughn." Johnson pulled her around to face him. "The .22 entered his back...close to his spine. You need to brace for the worst."

"I have to be with him."

Johnson let her go, even though she knew he had questions.

All the questions and reports would just have to wait.

As she followed the paramedics out of the house, she heard Johnson shout, "Where the hell is Gates?"

Chapter Fourteen

The hours had all run together.

Renee wasn't even sure what day it was.

Paul had been airlifted to Miami's Trauma Center. Some cop whose name she couldn't recall had driven her here despite the DEA's insistence that she stay behind and give her statement. Johnson had basically told the man in charge where to go and what to do when he got there. In his opinion, the DEA had enough to do figuring out what had happened to their man Gates, who had conveniently disappeared. At least now Renee understood how Victor had known when to precisely plan his moves.

She could truthfully say that she was glad that bastard was dead.

Over and over, her mind had played Paul's last words to her. The idea that her deception was the last thought he had about her made the agony almost unbearable.

A neurosurgical team had started the process of removing the bullet three hours ago.

Paul was stable, but the prognosis was unknown.

The bullet from the .22 had entered at an angle, lodging close to the spine. Apparently when Paul had stood up, the bullet had moved closer, pressing against nerves, paralyzing his upper body and making breathing difficult.

Grief so overwhelming rushed over her each time she thought of it that her stomach clenched mercilessly. He couldn't die. He just couldn't.

She remembered what he'd said about his previous back injury, about how he was glad it had been low on his spine so that there was no risk to his arms and hands. Surely God wouldn't take that from him now.

She closed her eyes and fought back the tears.

"Vaughn."

She opened her eyes to find that Jim Colby had sat down beside her. He'd arrived a few hours ago.

She dabbed at her eyes with a tissue and took a deep breath. "Hey."

"Any news yet?"

She shook her head.

"I wanted to let you know that I tracked down the admin clerk who changed the hospital records in Mexico City. The hospital's attorney has already faxed a statement to the DEA that Paul Reyes was the one who had the surgery, not Victor."

"Does that clear up any questions?"

"Yes. The case against Victor Reyes is officially closed. Apparently he had been planning to take over his brother's life for several months. The newly elected Mexican president was considering allowing Victor's extradition. Gates gave in to Victor's persuasion when the price was right. The bastard actually talked Darla Stewart into coming to us for help to set this whole thing in motion. Paul was to be the scapegoat."

Renee's jaw hardened with hatred. She hoped Victor Reyes burned in hell. She hoped Gates got what he deserved, as well.

Before she could say as much to Jim, the door opened and one of the doctors who had spoken to her before the surgery entered the small waiting room.

She pushed to her feet. Jim stood next to her.

"How did it go?" Please, she prayed, let him be okay.

"He came through the surgery very well," Dr. Kilpatrick explained, his tone cautious.

"Any permanent damage?" Jim asked the question she couldn't bear to utter.

Dr. Kilpatrick considered his words carefully. "It's difficult to tell at this point. The swelling obscures the issue. There was no structural damage to the spine, which is very good. However, we have to assume since sensory control, including the involuntary act of breathing, was hampered, that there may have been enough pressure to cause bruising. Frankly, this can go either way. He may recover without any permanent damage, or he may not. Only time will tell. Could be hours, could be days, before we know for certain."

Jim asked a few more questions and thanked the doctor. Renee couldn't stop thinking about how devastated Paul would be if he couldn't paint anymore.

Would he even want to live if that turned out to be the case?

"When can I see him?" she asked before the doctor could get away.

"Not for a while yet," Kilpatrick said gently. "Someone will come for you when he's awake and able to take visitors."

When the doctor had gone, she dropped back into her chair, her legs unable to hold up her weight any longer.

Jim resumed his seat beside her. "Would you like me to make a fresh pot of coffee?"

The current pot had scorched on the warming plate.

She shook her head. "No thanks."

"You did a good job, Vaughn."

Somehow it felt as if she'd failed. Sure they'd got Victor, but Paul was…seriously injured.

"If you hadn't warned me about Victor's plan,

Gates would have taken Paul down. We wouldn't be here. We'd be at the morgue."

She shuddered. "Was that the plan?" She turned to Jim. "To execute Victor Reyes without a trial?" Not that she actually gave a damn, but the wrong man had been targeted.

"According to the agent who assumed control of the case after Gates disappeared, they were only going to take Victor out if he didn't surrender voluntarily. We had no way of knowing Victor had a little setup of his own."

None of those final moments she'd witnessed made sense. "I'm still unclear about how Paul ended up with a gun?"

"Felipe Santos, one of Victor's personal bodyguards, spilled his guts for a deal. He says Victor set the whole thing up. He had two weapons on him as the sting went down. A .38, which he forced Paul to take when they hugged. Apparently he knew Paul wouldn't try to shoot him unless he forced the issue."

"That's why he dragged me into Paul's line of sight at that moment," she realized out loud.

"Right," Jim confirmed. "Victor had taped the second weapon, the .22, to his side beneath his shirt in case things went wrong. He had no intention of letting his brother survive."

All the hatred she felt for the man came rushing back. She rubbed her forehead, didn't want to hear any more of this. She just wanted good news about Paul.

"They haven't located Gates yet?"

Jim shook his head. "They will. Don't worry."

She prayed he was right.

"Why don't I go get you something to eat?" Jim offered.

She was relatively certain that she couldn't eat, but she appreciated the offer. "I'm okay for now."

"All right, then." He leaned back in his seat. "We'll just wait it out."

And that was what they did. Jim Colby sat right there beside her for hours…too many to count. Conversation was sporadic, but just having him there helped.

Exhaustion had gotten the better of Renee and she'd dozed off when the door to the private waiting room finally opened once more.

A nurse offered a smile when Renee looked up.

"Can I see him now?" Renee was on her feet and at the door before she had cleared the haze of sleep from her head. Her pulse tripped into triple time.

"Ms. Vaughn, Dr. Kilpatrick wanted me to let you know that Mr. Reyes is awake and breathing completely on his own now."

Renee's knees went weak with relief. "That's great. Can I see him?" she repeated, wondering why the nurse just didn't take her to him.

"You can, but it's imperative that he not move and that he not be overexcited."

Renee nodded. "I understand."

Jim gave her a nod. "I'll wait here for you."

She followed the nurse to the ICU. Paul's cubicle was directly across from the nurse's station. The glass walls allowed a full visual on all patients in the unit.

"We can only give you five minutes, Ms. Vaughn."

Renee would take whatever she got.

She moved up next to Paul's bed. "Hey," she said softly as she took his hand in hers.

He opened his eyes. "Hey." His voice was rusty. He licked his lips.

"The doctors say you're doing great." She smiled, fighting hard to keep the tears at bay.

"That's what they tell me."

He looked so unnaturally pale. Her heart squeezed. "I can only stay five minutes. But I'll be back as often as they'll allow." That his fingers remained limp in hers filled her stomach with dread.

"Tell me quickly," he murmured, his voice so low she could barely hear it.

"Tell you what?" She caressed his jaw. Wished she could crawl into the bed with him and just hold him close. He looked so vulnerable.

"Who are you? I must know."

That ache welled inside her. "My name is Renee Vaughn. I work for the Equalizers." She shrugged. "It's sort of a private investigations firm."

His brow wrinkled in confusion. "You were investigating me?"

She bit her lip for a second, then told him the truth. "Your brother. We were investigating Victor."

"You needed me to get to him." As dull as his dark eyes were from the injury and the surgery, she could see the regret and disappointment glimmering there.

"Yes."

He took a deep breath. The harsh movement worried her. Was he okay? Had she upset him?

"I am very tired now." He closed his eyes.

She pressed a kiss to his forehead and placed his hand back on the sheet.

There was nothing else she could say. If he never wanted to see her again, she would have no choice but to understand. He'd been dealing with betrayal and deception his whole life. She doubted if he wanted any more of it intruding in his life.

"I'm sorry, Ms. Vaughn," the nurse said from the door, "that's all the time for now."

Renee thanked her and left the cubicle. As promised, Jim Colby waited for her outside the ICU.

"There's a U.S. Marshal waiting." He gestured in the direction of the private waiting room for family members of surgical patients. "He's says that it's urgent that he speak with you."

Bewildered, she met his gaze. "I don't understand."

"It's about your brother, Vaughn. You need to do this. I'll be right here. If anything changes I'll let you know."

Embassy Suites Hotel, Miami
9:00 p.m.

RENEE HESITATED outside Room 618. She wasn't sure she wanted to know anything else about her brother. For two years she'd been told she couldn't go near him—orders that came straight from him. He didn't want her anywhere near him. No matter what new evidence she uncovered, she was not to speak of it. There was nothing she could do but stay away. So she'd done just that. She'd left Texas and tried to start over in Atlanta.

She couldn't imagine why anyone on her brother's case would come all the way to Miami or would want to talk to her. Or why the hell she would bother letting them bring her here.

"He's waiting, Ms. Vaughn."

Renee looked up at the marshal standing next to her. He'd been kind and patient as she ranted about her reasons for not wanting to ever hear her brother's name again. He'd known she was reacting on emotion.

She squared her shoulders and took a deep breath. "All right." Jim had arranged for her to have a shower at the hospital, and he'd rounded up new clothes for her hours ago. So she looked halfway respectable, not that it mattered. She wasn't here to impress anyone, frankly she didn't know why the hell she was here.

Marshal Farnsworth rapped on the door twice and it opened. A stern-looking man in a dark suit, with the same demeanor as Farnsworth, stared at her, then glanced at the man next to her. "We're ready."

Ready? Ready for what? Just what the hell was going on here?

Marshal Farnsworth nodded.

"Come in, Ms. Vaughn," the other man said as he moved away from the door.

Her heart had started to pound by the time the door was closed behind her. Had her brother been executed while she was out of reach? She'd scarcely had time to think about the situation as she'd run for her life. Now that he was dead, did they want to hear about her theories regarding her brother's innocence? That didn't make sense. Unless they suspected wrongdoing. A little late for that.

"This is highly unusual," the unidentified man started off, "but your brother was insistent."

"Ma'am, this is Marshal Owens," Farnsworth said. "We're transitioning Matthew."

She was totally lost now. "What are you talking about?"

"Please, sit down." Owens motioned to a chair in the room's sitting area.

The room was a suite. From the doors on either side of the room, she'd say a two-bedroom suite.

She sat. The quicker this was over, the sooner she could get back to Paul.

"I'm going to let your brother fill you in, then we

have to go. The longer we stay here, the greater the risk."

The idea that he'd said her brother had stunned her, she barely heard the rest of what he had to say. Her brother was sitting on death row in a Texas prison…wasn't he?

The two marshals stepped out into the hall, leaving her alone. The door to one of the bedrooms opened and her brother appeared.

"Hey, sis."

The fury that rose so rapidly was irrational, but something over which she had no control. She sprang to her feet. "What's going on here, Matthew?"

He was out?

Alive?

More incredible, he was speaking to her?

He walked over and hugged her. At first she stood there, her arms limp, her thoughts churning wildly, and then instinct took over. She hugged her brother fiercely, battled back the tears she refused to shed for him yet again.

He drew back. "I don't have much time, so I'll be brief."

They sat down and she listened as her brother told her an incredible tale of fear and desperation. He'd confessed to the murders of two of Austin's socially elite only because he'd had no choice. When Renee had learned the truth and attempted to help him, the threat shifted to her. That was the reason he'd pushed her out of his life—to protect her. Unbeknownst to the real killer, a man key to a Mafia-like organization in Texas, Matthew had started cooperating with the FBI. Since Renee had been out of his life and out of Texas for two years, all deemed that it would be safe for her. As of midnight the night before, Matthew Vaughn was dead, executed in a Texas prison. The Mafia in Texas was under investigation and already a dozen had been indicted, including the man who'd terrorized Renee and her brother—the real murderer.

It was over.

There was just one problem.

Matthew had to go into the Witness Protection Program. This would be the last time Renee ever saw her brother.

10:38 p.m.

RENEE WAS EXHAUSTED by the time Marshal Farnsworth dropped her off at the hospital's lobby entrance. She wasn't sure how she would ever talk the nurses into allowing her to see Paul at this hour, but she had to try. Jim Colby had promised to stay. He'd given her his cell phone and would have called if Paul's condition had changed.

She and her brother had cleared the air between them. They'd laughed and cried and, most importantly, made peace. She had assured him that she would be safe with Jim Colby. She'd never met a man quite like him before. His firm was aptly named— the Equalizers. Jim Colby evened the odds for those who had nowhere else to turn. It wouldn't matter how the DEA handled their investigation; she'd lay odds that Jim Colby would see to it that Joseph Gates was found. Just as he had seen to it that the marshals treated her brother with the utmost care and respect. Though the investigation into her brother's case had already been ongoing, the Colby name had ensured that Matthew got what he deserved—a second chance.

For the first time in a long time, Renee smiled a real smile. She was proud to be a part of Jim's group. She was proud of her brother.

She headed across the lobby for the bank of elevators. If she hadn't been lost in thought, maybe she could have avoided the collision with another visitor.

"Excuse me." She looked up at the man with whom she'd collided.

Gates.

"This way, Vaughn."

She didn't have to see the weapon in his jacket pocket; she felt it nudging into her ribs.

"I didn't think you were this stupid, Gates."

"Shut up and move," he muttered as he ushered her in the direction of the hospital's parking garage.

"If I were in your shoes I'd be deep in Mexico or some other place where the law couldn't reach."

He didn't respond, just kept ushering her forward. The corridor was deserted, which meant the parking garage would be, as well. There were probably security cameras, but those wouldn't help her a whole lot. Someone would view the tape later and determine that yes, indeed, she had been kidnapped and/or murdered by Gates. But she'd be dead.

The one thing she knew for certain was that she could not allow him to get her into a vehicle.

The double doors that separated the hospital from the garage slid open, and he pushed her forward. The smell of gasoline and oil filled her nostrils. She had to think fast.

"You believe having a hostage is going to assure your safe passage?" she suggested. "You've seen too many movies, Gates. You should know better than that."

He slammed her against the passenger side of a car. He laughed. "No, Vaughn, this isn't about safe passage." He leaned his face close to hers. "This is about payback. I want Paul Reyes to know what his failure to cooperate cost him."

She was the one laughing now. "Come on. You think he cares about me? I was working under cover, using him. He knows that now. He won't care if you kill me."

Gates jerked the car door open. "Oh, yes, he'll care. I saw the way he protected you. He's lying in that hospital bed right now because he took a bullet for you."

Now or never.

She was dead for sure if she didn't try.

Throwing all her weight behind the move, she slammed her elbow into his gut.

He grunted, bent forward.

She twisted out of his hold.

She ran.

He grabbed her by the hair, jerked her backward. The pistol's barrel rammed into her temple. "Don't make me kill you here."

He shoved her into the front seat. "Scoot over. You're driving."

As she took her time sliding across the bench seat, she scanned the interior of the car for a weapon. She needed something…anything.

The keys.

She yanked the key out of the switch before she'd slid behind the wheel. She turned on the man settling into the passenger seat. With her left hand, she shoved at the weapon. She stabbed the key into the side of his neck, going for an artery.

The pistol discharged.

The windshield shattered.

She was straddling him, struggling to keep the pistol away from her head. Blood squirted from his neck…splattered across her face. Another explosion from the pistol. The bullet whizzed past her ear. Too close.

If she could hold him down…

Twist the key in his neck…

He screamed.

They fell out of the car onto the concrete floor.

"Don't move!"

She didn't have time to look up, had to hold Gates off her.

A foot came down on top of the hand still clutching the gun.

Renee looked up, still struggling to hold Gates away from her.

Sam Johnson.

Gates collapsed on top of her.

His eyes were open, unblinking.

Damn. She rolled him off her and scrambled up.

Johnson toed the gun free from Gates's limp fingers. "Guess you'd better go in there and tell 'em you've got one for the morgue."

Renee nodded.

She'd killed a man.

Johnson steadied her when she swayed. "It was you or him, Vaughn. Don't sweat it."

She was still nodding, somehow unable to stop the bobbing of her head.

Security flooded the garage. E.R. personnel rushed in to attempt to resuscitate Gates, but it was too late. Just as well. The bastard didn't deserve to live. He belonged in hell with his friend Victor.

Johnson gave his statement to a cop while she was

questioned by another. She didn't remember the cops arriving. Time seemed to be on fast-forward and she couldn't catch up.

The DEA arrived.

Renee learned that Jim Colby had ordered Johnson to keep an eye on her, just in case Gates did exactly what he'd done. She'd have to thank Jim later.

Right now, she just wanted to see Paul.

6:00 a.m.

ONCE THE POLICE and the DEA were through questioning her, Jim had forced her to get some sleep. Her statement was confirmed by the hospital's security cameras, so she was in the clear. Johnson had brought her yet another change of clothes and she showered, washing away the traitor's blood. Then she admitted defeat and slept in the nurses' lounge.

She hadn't wanted to, but Jim had insisted. ICU rules wouldn't allow her to see Paul until six this morning.

The idea that she'd had to kill Gates still seemed on the fringes of reality. Jim told her that the shock would wear off, and reality would set in later. She would need counseling. He knew someone who could help her work through it. Right now, she was just glad it was over.

Her heart was running away in her chest as she neared Paul's cubicle in the ICU. She wanted to see him desperately. Wanted to tell him that she hadn't intended to hurt him in any way. But she was scared to death he would tell her to go away and never come back.

For once in her life, everything was fixed. She had a new career that made her feel that what she did mattered. She and her brother had made amends. They both deserved to live happily ever after. But her happily ever after hinged completely on this man.

He was awake.

"I understand there was excitement last night," he said, his voice not quite so rusty this morning.

She nodded. "Gates is dead."

"Good."

Renee stood at his bedside, but this time she didn't reach for his hand.

"You look much better this morning," she offered in a cheery tone that sounded fake even to her.

He was watching her, assessing what he saw. She resisted the impulse to look away. She had to face whatever his decision turned out to be. No more running away. She'd done enough of that. She'd run away from Texas to escape the reality of what had happened between her and her brother. She'd run away from Atlanta because she couldn't deal with the trust necessary to prosecute a case again. She'd tried to fit in again—to belong to the world of politics and prosecution in Atlanta's high-profile DA's office, but she just couldn't. The past kept coming back to haunt her…making her doubt her esteemed colleagues… making her doubt herself.

No more running away.

He reached up, caressed her cheek with his fingertips. She leaned into his touch. Then he smiled. "I'm glad you're safe." He lowered his hand back to the bed, the movement seeming to have cost him a great deal of strength.

It hit her then. He'd moved his arm. Touched her face. Hope bloomed in her chest.

His answering smile melted the ice of fear that had chilled her. "They say I'll make a full recovery."

Tears slid down her cheeks before she could stop them. "That's great. Really great."

He placed his hand on hers where she clutched the bed's side rail. "It's time you properly introduced yourself to me."

Relief gushed through her. "Renee Vaughn, from Texas, originally."

"Well, Renee Vaughn from Texas, we have much to talk about." He squeezed her hand. "Many plans to make."

She leaned down and placed a soft kiss on his lips. "Many plans."

Their gazes locked, and he looked at her with all the passion that she'd seen when he was making love to her. "First thing, I want to paint you."

She bit her lower lip to stop its trembling. "I think that can be arranged."

She kissed him again, this time with a definite promise of things to come.

Chapter Fifteen

Jim Colby parked in front of his house and exhaled a heavy breath.

He had missed dinner with his girls again.

Today had been a busy one for a Saturday. Several new cases had come in. Pretty soon, he would need to hire an additional associate if Tasha opted not to join him at work.

Not that he could blame her. The idea of leaving their daughter in the hands of anyone besides close family was something neither of them was prepared to consider.

He went inside and locked the door.

The house was quiet.

He was sure Tasha had left dinner for him, but he was too tired to eat.

As quietly as he could, he trudged up the stairs.

He peeked in his daughter's room and, as tired as he was, he smiled down at her. So sweet, so beautiful. Just like her mother.

He eased out of her room and went to the bedroom where his wife would likely be asleep, as well. He peeled off his clothes and slid beneath the sheet and snuggled up to her backside. It felt good to lie down; having her sweet body close was just icing on the cake. He was still amazed that she loved him. That their child was so perfect...that his life was real.

Tasha turned over and sighed contentedly. "You're home."

"Mmm-hmm." God, she smelled good. He nuzzled her neck.

"Your daughter said da-da tonight."

Jim's heart constricted. "Seriously?"

"Seriously."

And he'd missed it.

"Don't worry," she stroked his jaw, "I got it on video."

"Thank you." He kissed her forehead. What else was he going to miss?

"Victoria was here."

He stilled.

"She's worried about you, Jim. She thinks you're working too hard. Some of the cases you're taking are pretty dangerous."

"Starting right now," he said, ushering her beneath him, "I promise I will not come home later than seven. And I will be more selective about the cases I take." If he didn't, his mother was going to move into the office with him. Already, she stopped in two or three times each week, checking on him and assessing the cases he accepted. As much as he loved her, her concern was moving into the interference zone. They were going to have to have a serious talk. He was a grown man; he didn't need his mother looking over his shoulder.

"Good. I like having you home for dinner." Tasha looped her arms around his neck. "Just remember, Victoria loves you. She wants to protect you, just like we want to protect Jamie."

"Except," he murmured against her neck, "I don't need protecting. I'm a big boy."

Tasha moved against him. "I can see that."

He pushed the regrets and worries aside and made love to his wife. Right now was all that mattered.

Tomorrow would take care of itself.

He would see to it.

And Victoria would just have to get used to the idea that her son could take care of himself.

End of story.

* * * * *

MEDITERRANEAN NIGHTS

Join the guests and crew of **Alexandra's Dream**, *the newest luxury ship to set sail on the romantic Mediterranean, as they experience the glamorous world of cruising.*

A new Harlequin continuity series begins in June 2007 with
FROM RUSSIA, WITH LOVE
by Ingrid Weaver

Marina Artamova books a cabin on the luxurious cruise ship **Alexandra's Dream,** *when she finds out that her orphaned nephew and his adoptive father are aboard. She's determined to be reunited with the boy...but the romantic ambience of the ship and her undeniable attraction to a man she considers her enemy are about to interfere with her quest!*

Turn the page for a sneak preview!

Piraeus, Greece

"THERE SHE IS, Stefan. *Alexandra's Dream*." David Anderson squatted beside his new son and pointed at the dark blue hull that towered above the pier. The cruise ship was a majestic sight, twelve decks high and as long as a city block. A circle of silver and gold stars, the logo of the Liberty Cruise Line, gleamed from the swept-back smokestack. Like some legendary sea creature born for the water, the ship emanated power from every sleek curve—even at rest it held the promise of motion. "That's going to be our home for the next ten days."

The child beside him remained silent, his cheeks working in and out as he sucked furiously on his thumb. Hair so blond it appeared white ruffled against his forehead in the harbor breeze. The baby-sweet scent unique to the very young mingled with the tang of the sea.

"Ship," David said. "Uh, *parakhod*."

From beneath his bangs, Stefan looked at the *Alexandra's Dream*. Although he didn't release his thumb, the corners of his mouth tightened with the beginning of a smile.

David grinned. That was Stefan's first smile this afternoon, one of only two since they had left the orphanage yesterday. It was probably because of the boat—according to the orphanage staff, the boy loved boats, which was the main reason David had decided to book this cruise. Then again, there was a strong possibility the smile could have been a reaction to David's attempt at pocket-dictionary Russian. Whatever the cause, it was a good start.

The liaison from the adoption agency had claimed that Stefan had been taught some English, but David had yet to see evidence of it. David continued to speak, positive his son would understand his tone even if he couldn't grasp the words. "This is her maiden voyage. Her first trip, just like this is our first trip, and that makes it special." He motioned toward the stage that had been set up on the pier beneath the ship's bow. "That's why everyone's celebrating."

The ship's official christening ceremony had been held the day before and had been a closed affair, with only the cruise-line executives and VIP guests invited, but the stage hadn't yet been disassembled. Banners bearing the blue and white of the Greek flag of the ship's owner, as well as the Liberty circle-of-stars logo, draped the edges of the platform. In the center, a group of musicians and a dance troupe dressed in traditional white folk costumes performed for the benefit of the *Alexandra's Dream*'s first passengers. Their audience was in a festive mood, snapping their fingers in time to the music while the dancers twirled and wove through their steps.

David bobbed his head to the rhythm of the mandolins. They were playing a folk tune that seemed vaguely familiar, possibly from a movie he'd seen. He hummed a few notes. "Catchy melody, isn't it?"

Stefan turned his gaze on David. His eyes were a striking shade of blue, as cool and pale as a winter horizon and far too solemn for a child not yet five. Still, the smile that hovered at the corners of his mouth persisted. He moved his head with the music, mirroring David's motion.

David gave a silent cheer at the interaction. Hopefully, this cruise would provide countless opportunities for more. "Hey, good for you," he said. "Do you like the music?"

The child's eyes sparked. He withdrew his thumb with a pop. *"Moozika!"*

"Music. Right!" David held out his hand. "Come on, let's go closer so we can watch the dancers."

Stefan grasped David's hand quickly, as if he feared it would be withdrawn. In an instant his budding smile was replaced by a look close to panic.

Did he remember the car accident that had killed

his parents? It would be a mercy if he didn't. As far as David knew, Stefan had never spoken of it to anyone. Whatever he had seen had made him run so far from the crash that the police hadn't found him until the next day. The event had traumatized him to the extent that he hadn't uttered a word until his fifth week at the orphanage. Even now he seldom talked.

David sat back on his heels and brushed the hair from Stefan's forehead. That solemn, too-old gaze locked with his, and for an instant, David felt as if he looked back in time at an image of himself thirty years ago.

He didn't need to speak the same language to understand exactly how this boy felt. He knew what it meant to be alone and powerless among strangers, trying to be brave and tough but wishing with every fiber of his being for a place to belong, to be safe, and most of all for someone to love him....

He knew in his heart he would be a good parent to Stefan. It was why he had never considered halting the adoption process after Ellie had left him. He hadn't balked when he'd learned of the recent claim by Stefan's spinster aunt, either; the absentee relative had shown up too late for her case to be considered. The adoption was meant to be. He and this child already shared a bond that went deeper than paperwork or legalities.

A seagull screeched overhead, making Stefan start and press closer to David.

"That's my boy," David murmured. He swallowed hard, struck by the simple truth of what he had just said.

That's my *boy.*

"I CAN'T BE PATIENT, RUDOLPH. I'm not going to stand by and watch my nephew get ripped from his country and his roots to live on the other side of the world."

Rudolph hissed out a slow breath. "Marina, I don't like the sound of that. What are you planning?"

"I'm going to talk some sense into this American kidnapper."

"No. Absolutely not. No offence, but diplomacy is not your strong suit."

"Diplomacy be damned. Their ship's due to sail at five o'clock."

"Then you wouldn't have an opportunity to speak with him even if his lawyer agreed to a meeting."

"I'll have ten days of opportunities, Rudolph, since I plan to be on board that ship."

* * * * *

*Follow Marina and David as they join forces
to uncover the reason behind little Stefan's
unusual silence, and the secret behind the death
of his parents....*

*Look for FROM RUSSIA, WITH LOVE
by Ingrid Weaver
in stores June 2007.*

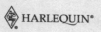

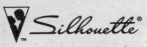

Silhouette®

ROMANTIC SUSPENSE

**Sparked by Danger,
Fueled by Passion.**

*This month and every month look for
four new heart-racing romances
set against a backdrop of suspense!*

Available in June 2007

Shelter from the Storm
by **RaeAnne Thayne**

A Little Bit Guilty
(Midnight Secrets miniseries)
by **Jenna Mills**

Mob Mistress
by **Sheri WhiteFeather**

A Serial Affair
by **Natalie Dunbar**

Available wherever you buy books!

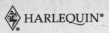
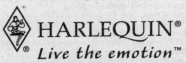

REQUEST YOUR FREE BOOKS!

2 FREE NOVELS PLUS 2 FREE GIFTS!

HARLEQUIN®

INTRIGUE®

Breathtaking Romantic Suspense

YES! Please send me 2 FREE Harlequin Intrigue® novels and my 2 FREE gifts. After receiving them, if I don't wish to receive any more books, I can return the shipping statement marked "cancel." If I don't cancel, I will receive 6 brand-new novels every month and be billed just $4.24 per book in the U.S., or $4.99 per book in Canada, plus 25¢ shipping and handling per book and applicable taxes, if any*. That's a savings of close to 15% off the cover price! I understand that accepting the 2 free books and gifts places me under no obligation to buy anything. I can always return a shipment and cancel at any time. Even if I never buy another book from Harlequin, the two free books and gifts are mine to keep forever.

182 HDN EEZ7   382 HDN EEZK

Name	(PLEASE PRINT)	
Address		Apt. #
City	State/Prov.	Zip/Postal Code

Signature (if under 18, a parent or guardian must sign)

Mail to the Harlequin Reader Service®:
IN U.S.A.: P.O. Box 1867, Buffalo, NY 14240-1867
IN CANADA: P.O. Box 609, Fort Erie, Ontario L2A 5X3

Not valid to current Harlequin Intrigue subscribers.

Want to try two free books from another line?
Call 1-800-873-8635 or visit www.morefreebooks.com.

* Terms and prices subject to change without notice. NY residents add applicable sales tax. Canadian residents will be charged applicable provincial taxes and GST. This offer is limited to one order per household. All orders subject to approval. Credit or debit balances in a customer's account(s) may be offset by any other outstanding balance owed by or to the customer. Please allow 4 to 6 weeks for delivery.

Your Privacy: Harlequin is committed to protecting your privacy. Our Privacy Policy is available online at www.eHarlequin.com or upon request from the Reader Service. From time to time we make our lists of customers available to reputable firms who may have a product or service of interest to you. If you would prefer we not share your name and address, please check here. ☐

HI07

HARLEQUIN®

American ROMANCE®

is proud to present a special treat this
Fourth of July with three stories
to kick off your summer!

SUMMER LOVIN'
by
Marin Thomas,
Laura Marie Altom
Ann Roth

This year, celebrating the Fourth of July in Silver Cliff,
Colorado, is going to be special. There's an all-year
high school reunion taking place before the old
school building gets torn down. As old flames find
each other and new romances begin, this small
town is looking like the perfect place
for some summer lovin'!

Available June 2007
wherever Harlequin books are sold.

www.eHarlequin.com   HAR75169

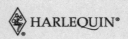

COMING NEXT MONTH

#993 HIGH SOCIETY SABOTAGE by Kathleen Long
Bodyguards Unlimited, Denver, CO (Book 4 of 6)
In order to blend into the world of CEO Stephen Turner, PPS agent
Sara Montgomery adopts the role she left behind years ago—
debutante—to stop investors from dying.

#994 ROYAL LOCKDOWN by Rebecca York
Lights Out (Book 1 of 4)
A *brand-new continuity!* Princess Ariana LeBron brought the famous
Beau Pays sapphire to Boston, which security expert Shane Peters
intended to steal. But plans changed when an act of revenge plunged
Boston into a complete blackout.

#995 COLBY VS. COLBY by Debra Webb
Colby Agency: The Equalizers (Book 3 of 3)
Does the beginning of the Equalizers mean the end of the Colby
Agency? Jim Colby and Victoria Camp-Colby go head-to-head when
they both send agents to L.A., where nothing is as simple as it seems.

#996 SECRET OF DEADMAN'S COULEE by B.J. Daniels
Whitehorse, Montana
A downed plane in Missouri Breaks badlands was bad enough. But on
board was someone who was murdered thirty-two years ago? Sheriff
Carter Jackson and Eve Bailey thought their reunion would be hard
enough....

#997 SHOWDOWN WITH THE SHERIFF by Jan Hambright
Sheriff Logan Brewer called Rory Matson back to Reaper's Point, not
to identify her father's body, but the skull discovered in his backpack
at the time of his death.

#998 FORBIDDEN TEMPTATION by Paula Graves
Women were dying in Birmingham's trendy nightclub district, and only
Rose Browning saw a killer's pattern emerging. But she didn't know
how to stop him, not until hot-shot criminal profiler Daniel Hartman
arrived.